Jackdaw & Other Stories

by the same author

Betrothal (together with *Fidelity*)
two novellas: Brynmill Press 978 0 907839 59 0

[with Richard Shepheard]
George Borrow: the Dingle Chapters:
    an Introduction, a Reprint, a Biographical
    Conundrum:
Brynmill Press 978 0 907839 63 7

Jackdaw
&
Other Stories

M. B. Mencher

DURRANT PUBLISHING

copyright © 2008 M. B. Mencher
first published 2008 by
Durrant Publishing, Norfolk, England
book design by the author
typeset by The Brynmill Press Ltd
Printed and bound by Lightning Source

ISBN   978-1-905946-03-7

British Library Cataloguing in Publication Data: a
catalogue record of this book is available from the
British Library.

The right of M. B. Mencher to be identified as the
author of this work has been asserted by him in
accordance with the Copyright, Designs and Patents
Act 1988.

www.durrantpublishing.co.uk

Contents

For friends, near and far

A Cup of Coffee

"We started off in one bed, then we had twin beds, then he slept downstairs, now he's in Brighton!"

The little woman, with the red Caucasian hat, smiled and the young man looked deep into her cloudy brown eyes which were still lovely.

"So you had lovers?"

"Oh, many lovers. I have lived in Paradise, you know. Well, at the beginning of each affair. But then I knew when my men were going to leave me. I could see it in their eyes. Men are such fools! They imagine we don't know."

She laughed.

"Oh yes. And then there was the long period of rest."

"Of rest?"

"Eight years. Yes, I slept for eight years. They tried to wake me up—with 'shock treatment' and such-like. It was absurd. Bloody silly!"

The expression sounded wrong in her foreign voice.

"Sleep. I watched the bloody silly television and read scores and scores of pages of trash every day. My work was ruined. I could do nothing. But then I woke up and my life became full of activity. Much fuller than yours is."

There seemed no point in arguing with her.

"My husband. He was a queer man. Oh yes. Do you know what he did? He made me paint my face, inches thick—"

She made a little gesture, at the side of her face, with her hand, signifying disgust.

"—and I had to wear tight skirts. So tight! And I had to stand at Piccadilly Circus until some man tried to pick me up. Then my husband would walk up and say, 'I'm sorry, this is my wife!' It made him feel so good to know that other men wanted me. I don't think he wanted me himself. But afterwards, we would go home and make love."

She laughed again.

"But it is a long time ago now. How old are you?"

"Thirty-nine."

"Oh, thirty-nine. And how old do you think I am? I'm sixty-six and I don't care who knows it. I know a lot of young men."

She was petite, yet plump, and wore a long summer dress, with a necklace of beans, yes beans, round her throat. One of her boyfriends, she said, had given her the necklace. It was very attractive. And she had the little, round, velvet hat, red, with nice embroidery on it.

"What is your work then?" the young man asked.

"I'm a photographer, a famous photographer. I represent England at international exhibitions. I photograph nudes."

He wondered for a moment whether she wanted to photograph him.

"Will you come to my house?"

"Well, that would be very nice," he said.

"Yes. Tell me," she said, getting out a little book from her handbag, "what is your address?"

"I do like your hat," he said.

She laughed.

"Don't change the subject," she said, opening the little book and getting ready to write.

He gave his address in a slightly incorrect form, so that she would not be able to trace him; and he wrote down her address on a paper serviette.

And he wondered how much of what she had said was true and whether she was simply a sad old lady trying desperately to maintain an illusion of her sexual potency. Or perhaps she was as well supplied with admirers as she claimed. But, as he looked, deep, into her deep-brown eyes, he thought how lovely they were, how they shone with life, and how they were eyes made in the image of God's eyes—and how they resembled the eyes of his mother.

Neighbours

1 *Cosy*

She was fair, pale-cheeked, with a slightly twisted mouth, the lips thin, and she painted dead flowers, ruins, and wilting ladies. She would walk for hours in Victorian cemeteries, gazing at the dying flowers, the neglected headstones, the silent mounds. For these people, swathing themselves in black lace, chiffon, grown fat with the unhealthy lives they led, had prepared eagerly for death, preserving amidst the trivia of their ceremonious lives a solemnity that unfitted them for angels' wings but permitted them to sit heavily on the right-hand side of God. Covering her shoulders with shawls and draping herself in dresses of purple silk whose hems brushed the floor, her eyes wide, she attended to the spirit world in stuffy rooms where weird things took place. So the thick tree in her painting was ephemeral, though every knob and gnarl was pictured, ephemeral as the wreath of weightless leaves, luminously tan, that tumbled from its branches and wound themselves in deadly fashion round the trunk, the canvas fading into whiteness at the edges.

They were sitting in a heavily furnished room which was lit by ornamental oil lamps. On the dark-green walls were posters by Mucha, a gilt-framed photograph of the Royal Family (taken in the 1860s) and a reproduction of Waterhouse's *Hylas and the Nymphs*. Cosily curled up on an embroidered cushion was a tortoiseshell cat which had been neutered.

Her hair seemed to soak up the soft light, gleaming blondly, and she was conscious of the shadows into which it threw the folds of her dress, varying the texture. The old lady opposite smiled, twitching her grey skirt before flipping over a page of the little blue book she held in her hand. Maliciously Haydon handed her another pastry from the delicately flowered plate, which she accepted courteously, for the young people enjoyed watching her stuff herself like a greedy baby.

What a relief now Adam had gone! If it hadn't been for his green corduroy jacket and intellectual face, they would never have invited him.

Haydon took the cat into his arms. The spoiled, tame thing lay back offering its white undercoat to his fingers, so he rubbed gently.

"I wish Sarah were here!" he sighed, ceasing to fondle.

"I think you play very beautifully yourself," said Miss Sadler, "though naturally you don't have Sarah's facility."

Matilda snorted her dissent from the first proposition.

"Oh, Miss Sadler, how can you compare . . . ?" Nevertheless he went to the piano and good-humouredly stumbled through a Chopin nocturne.

"Well, this has been a most enjoyable evening," said the old lady, rising awkwardly to her feet when he had finished playing, "but I mustn't keep my pussies waiting for their supper any longer."

"Don't go, Miss Sadler. Or feed your pussies first, then come back and have some more coffee."

She looked at him coyly. "Shall I?"

"Oh yes, do!"

"Very well." She gathered herself together and slowly shuffled towards the door. When she had gone Matilda looked daggers at the helpless boy.

Downstairs she re-entered the squalor she had left behind. The big kitchen table was covered with old newspapers upon which were tins of cat food in various states of demolition, their lids open and scraps of meat or fish spattered on the sides or yellowing newspaper. An overpowering stench rose from a tray underneath the sink, where a black cat was fastidiously covering its excreta. Another mewed its welcome to the old lady's quiet greetings.

She closed the door and felt the little beast leap on to her back, then, digging its claws into her clothing, climb up to her shoulder, thence to the top of her head. Carefully making her way to the fridge, Miss Sadler bent down once more and looked into the eyes of the other cat, who with tail up mewed insistently as she removed a bottle of milk. The first cat sprang to the top of the fridge, causing the old lady to emit a little scream as she felt the claws drive into her scalp, then jumped to the floor mewing by the side of its fellow. Soon they were contentedly lapping from different saucers.

It was then that Matilda conceived the idea of painting Miss Sadler's portrait. Flattered when told of it, the old lady was crestfallen when asked to sit in her old clothes in the midst of her kitchen.

2   *Morning*

Peeling and splitting peanuts for the birds, her hair escaping from the pins, she sat in a faded dressing gown before the table mess, Matilda balancing a canvas on her knees. In return the birds had sown the seeds of trees in her back garden, where no blade of grass grew. A gift of God.

Sarah rehearsed sections of a keyboard suite in the house next door, the sound sailing across to Miss Sadler's kitchen. Haydon did not hear the traffic in Trafalgar Square, thinking of Mucha as he strode along. Adam called his drawings cheap—the fool! They were exquisite. Sarah didn't like Chopin. Why didn't she like Chopin? Sarah was a kind of genius. Matilda was a genius too, and Miss Sadler a very gifted, funny old lady. As for himself? Ah, why could he achieve nothing? He could never carry anything through. He drifted. Why did he always and only drift? She would be painting now. What a scream! Miss Sadler sitting there in her torn old dressing gown, and she thought she was going to be painted as a fine lady. Poor Matilda: the smell of the cats. Foh! The remains of food, green with age and corruption. He would make a hot pot this evening. Some violets. Sheba should have some lightly poached fish. Poor thing wasn't feeling too well this morning. Perhaps it was the flea powder. Odious people!

Miles away Adam sat in the Staff Common-room, drinking coffee and talking. From the window, high up, he could see the estuary beyond the irregular contours of the town; the ancient cathedral and castle; a public park.

Why was no one talking to him this morning? He must learn to repress such symptoms of insecurity. Sometimes he was all extrovert. "If a man is self-conscious at thirty-seven, then it's obvious senile precocity." He remembered the sentence from a high-spirited little essay by D. H. Lawrence. It tickled him back to sanity.

Sarah was sobbing. Miss Sadler's transistor radio had begun to blare. So Sarah threw open her french window and set her radiogram at full blast. But Miss Sadler was partially deaf. Nevertheless, she saw Sarah standing behind a window with a face of thunderous grief. Soon the noise died down.

Matilda had had to leave because Miss Sadler informed her that her affairs were far too pressing to permit more than an hour or two of her time to be taken up in sitting for a portrait, and that only whilst she was able to do other necessary work, like shelling nuts for the birds. The cats had to be fed, as well as the birds, and . . . . But there was no point in drawing up a list.

Adam was flattered by the attentions of the girls he was teaching.
"So well-bred spaniels civilly delight
In mumbling of the game they dare not bite."
He was sure they thought him remarkably clever.

Haydon bought the bunch of violets.

3   *Evening*

How humiliated he felt, standing in the queue! And such a ragged queue, men straggling to one side, laughing, swearing, standing sullen or ashamed, wearing shabby overcoats. Positively he would not come here again, even if he went without the money. Mr Stokes from downstairs, who had received Unemployment Benefit for years, smiled at him compromisingly, as though he were Haydon's equal or even superior by virtue of greater experience, and enjoyed the prospect of his downfall; for Mr Stokes was an ignorant man, a Philistine. His room was a mess and he played the harmonica out of tune, keeping himself to himself. When he first took the room he told Miss Sadler (she said) that he was a "loner"; but that was no reason why he should splash the seat and floor of the lavatory when he emptied his pail of urine every morning. Ugh! the man was despicable. Nevertheless, he together with Miss Sadler made a good subject for comic anecdote when Sarah or Matilda, and Adam, came round.

Adam's soul was flooded with contempt as he thought of the people next door. Vanity, their lives were a vanity. Yet he valued their friendship. Even though they took no notice of him, he liked to sit in a deep armchair and bask in the comfort of their affected hospitality: dainty foods, malicious gossip, courtesies that amounted to stale gentilities —a self-conscious imitation of what they thought was a faded, lovelier world, the 1890s, yet a world they implicitly scorned too, by laughing at its excesses. Oh, how he felt the depravity of it all, Adam! But what else had he? He wished to move in a circle of brilliant like-minded spirits, and, when he did so, he was outshone. Hopeless, his case was hopeless. A case of ambition, vanity.

Miss Sadler had been "saved" twenty years ago, when she joined the Baptist Church.

4 *Necrophiliac*

The tombstones leaned eccentrically in the soft earth that was fertile in weeds, and big trees grew upward to the grey sky, their leafless branches extending over the decayed rubbish below—tin cans, rags, last year's leaves. Monumental tombs lined the main avenue to the crumbling Gothic chapel that smelt of urine, and a cat crept silently through the undergrowth. A few stragglers visited the fresh graves, but the cemetery was virtually abandoned by the living, containing last century's dead. Matilda loved the place, its unwholesomeness, its extravagance. For did not the overgrown inscriptions read: "Gone to sleep", "Beloved Dad", "We'll meet again", "After only five days' illness"? And hadn't the coffins been occasionally disturbed by Satanists? The refuse that had been dumped there spiced the solemnities with fitting irony, yet Matilda did not pity the dead or revile the living. She simply relished the complex sensations that the incongruous spectacle aroused in her. It was there for her, and it stimulated her artistic soul. Yet so desolate a place still owned the fresh buds of Spring on many a low bush, as well as the lurid bunches of cut flowers stuck in urn-like containers balanced on the chests of the sleeping earth-children, or flowers growing, with equally unnatural vividness in that gloomy spot, directly out of the earth-blankets. A General and his daughters were housed in one marble vault, whilst humbler folk inhabited the wooded hillside in their crazy inclinations. One vault stood empty with its doors swinging open, the shelves inside bare of coffins, but a pair of dirty ladies' tights swayed from the twigs of a bush nearby. Everywhere, tumbled in the earth, were marble "books" bearing the name and circumstances of forgotten souls. A lonely monument to Scottish martyrs encouraged a visitor to cherish freedom and, incidentally, reminded him that there was a world of action outside the defiled walls that, with their tottering ornamental pinnacles, surrounded the cemetery.

Miss Sadler's tombstone had already been designed at high cost, for she wished to be remembered by the passer-by who disturbed the obliterating ivy. But Matilda wanted a coffin of her own, to lie in when she was tired, in front of the sitting room fire. Haydon thought this a great joke, but Adam cringed, imagining that such a wish evinced an evil and decadent desire. But Miss Sadler's portrait grew wonderfully, whatever aberrations its executrice might seem to have. A ghostly figure sat "solid" on a kitchen chair, surrounded by material objects that belonged indisputably to this world, whilst she did not. The rubbish was not itself depicted, but a look of great sadness was on the sitter's face, which was bent downwards in the attitude she held when she was peeling peanuts—but there were no peanuts. Her figure was rendered in a shadowy blue, which was set off by the vivid, rather vulgar colours of kitchen utensils and cupboards; and the picture faded away at the edges into whiteness, falling short of the frame.

Matilda was not satisfied with it. She was never satisfied with her work. Poor Miss Sadler didn't know what to think. Neither did Sarah. Or Adam. Haydon, of course, was in raptures, but then he did have artistic inclinations himself, painting pretty flowers on lampshades, and such-like.

5 Performance

Beautiful the sculptured ceiling, painted white with gilt edgings, and the interior of the church was filled with light. At the piano sat Sarah, her face motioning gently to the music. She was nervous but the fingers did not betray her. On and on, with barely a pause, for forty minutes the music rolled out into the nave—the Goldberg Variations of Johann Sebastian Bach. Matilda held her breath in wonder, and Adam tried to stop himself being concerned about his wife's ordeal. But he had no need to worry. Even her attitude at the keyboard was classical in its simplicity. She had no affectations whatever. Haydon clasped his hands together in an expression of girlish enthusiasm. He turned to Matilda and beamed. A smile flickered in her eyes and she returned her concentration immediately and entirely to the music.

She had on a full-length black dress of damasked velvet which made her dark hair look coppery against it. It was too fine for the everyday street, but in London such anomalies are unexceptional. Matilda was arrayed in her purple splendour, the thin fair hair falling softly in a golden glow; and Haydon was dressed in his brown velvet, which he kept for special occasions, the hair of his head looking almost as lovely as Matilda's. Only Adam was out of place, in a dark suit.

Miss Sadler had stayed behind. She was getting too old to bestir herself greatly and no one had offered to give her a lift in his car. So she sat in the kitchen, combing fleas out of her cats and dropping the parasites, which she counted gleefully, into a basin of boiling water. Into her head, in the meantime, had come the idea for another poem— about the loveliness of music.

6   *Pussy*

Haydon's brother, Owen, had begun to pay attention to Matilda. He was a calligrapher and thorough Welshman, with pale blue discs for eyes that looked alien, as though he belonged to a semi-mythical race gifted with the second sight. But he scorned his brother's occultism and aestheticism. He was a sound businessman and sold his work cannily, though with a flourish of unworldly generosity. His hair grew wild at the temples, wavily tangled all over his head, and he dressed only in neutral colours—faded fawns and greys—to avoid clashing with any background and to avoid bruising the eye with brashness.

He treated Sarah with a familiarity to which she was unused, distrusting it but convinced of its innocence. It was only not innocent in encouraging a confidence which she did not see grounds for. But there was no question of his making "passes". Haydon envied his success with Matilda, though he did not want her for himself. He had such friends of his own sex, yet he preferred the company of women, in a general way.

It was Owen who had designed Miss Sadler's tombstone.

Adam was a menace. Not because Owen thought him a rival, but because he cast a Puritanical cloud over the company; whereas Haydon might contemplate anything but what was undecorative. Indecorum did not trouble him.

Owen kissed the cat. He lifted it to his face and nuzzled into its fur, then held it off to look into its impassive eyes. He laughed and the cat wriggled, so he set it on the floor. Then he caught it and rolled it over on to its back, rubbing its furry underside. It lay back in raptures. Then he picked it up again and began to talk at it, in caressing Welsh. Adam was piqued that he could not understand the words and marvelled at the other's little conquest. Sarah asked him to put it down, because she thought it wrong to make quite such a fuss of animals; but he brought it to her knee as a gift, and she was delighted. Matilda merely looked on. Then Adam stroked it sparingly, till it ran off the sofa and out of the room.

7 Spooky

Matthew moved in. How marvellously he played the piano or harmonium without reading a score! The cottage piano found a mate in the stocky organ, which shone respectably.

Miss Sadler welcomed this "marriage of true minds", sharing an enjoyment of hymns with the short, dark-haired man whose lips were red, and she would sing in her thin cracked voice to his secretly facetious accompaniment.

Owen didn't like him, finding himself encumbered with an ersatz brother, who couldn't at any rate speak Welsh, but he had to admit that Matthew made a good husband, managing the accounts and, presumably, completing the domestic life of his real brother. They were, Matthew and Haydon, fastidious to a fault. Matilda watched, wonderingly.

Great draughts of pleasure filled the sad soul as he pressed the organ-pedals and moulded with pliant fingers the yellowing keys. As a clerk in a shipping office he lived two lives, as did Adam, conversing with Miss Sadler who had, surprisingly, been in insurance herself. He, too, believed in the Afterlife, though as an extension of this one. There was no Heaven and no Hell, only an ethereal element where, like flowers under water, breathed the delighted spirits.

The zodiac turned round until Matilda's stars were in the ascendant, which was marked by the following paranormal event. A dumpy figure in a black dress and white veil attended the feast. Unfortunately, it was not Queen Victoria but Matthew disguised, so the initial shock was followed by laughter.

Rest in Peace

And so she spent her first night in the grave. It had been a fine February morning when they buried her. The light had grown stronger despite the ground-mist from the surrounding fields, so that the tombstones looked like a silent assembly of tottering soldiers, standing in the absolute quiet, for as yet the mourners had not arrived in their cars or on foot. The dead were getting ready to welcome her, when the open grave should be filled up. Just now it was standing empty, a deep trench supported by two planks along each of the longer sides, one of which planks was clearly beginning to bend under the strain of supporting the sandy earth it was meant to hold back; yet some earth had already fallen into the hole, and perhaps the whole grave would cave in if the burial did not take place in good time. But the mourners were beginning to arrive, and so the anxious gravedigger, in his woollen hat and jumper, breathed a sigh of relief.

The solemn service passed without a hitch, whilst Martha listened from within her beautifully fashioned coffin, with the bright brass fittings. She did not wish to get out, she did not wish to rejoin the world of the living, she was tired, she had lived enough.

Breathing was itself too much of an effort now. No, she was content to lie here quietly listening. It was quite a nice service, she thought; very dignified, simple, sincere. The one thing she would have liked to do was to get up and thank everyone for being so kind as to come here and maintain such a respectful silence. She would have made a joke about that. She had always had such a good sense of humour. But some people were weeping. How embarrassing! She wished she didn't have to hear that. But she could hear everything, she noticed with some surprise, and yes, she could actually hear what people were not saying! She could hear their thoughts. That was more embarrassing still. Dear God, this was too like being alive oneself. She must close her ears. She found that she could.

What was that? Oh yes, the eulogy. She had heard many a eulogy in her time, at the funerals she had attended; some of them true, some false. She hoped hers was true. But it wasn't for her to judge. She felt a tremor of fear. But where *was* her judge? *The* Judge? Surely she wasn't expected to judge herself? That was something she did only spasmodically whilst alive. She had once read a novel, she remembered, where the hero was judging himself the whole time, so much so that he veritably didn't have time to live. Surely that was not what a living soul was

supposed to do. Martha chuckled to herself.
But wasn't she being complacent? Oh dear,
she thought, this is all very well, lying here,
but what was in store? God Almighty and
the celestial trumpets, the awesome majesty
of the heavenly court! Well, so be it. She
would no more succumb to morbid anxiety
about that than she had when they first told
her she would die of a terrible disease.

Well, that was not quite true. No, she had
almost died then, at that moment; but when
they told her it was worth the fight, that she
might have years of life to live, if they managed
to hold the disease in check (for it was
incurable)—well, then she decided she would
assert herself above her fate and fight back.
Her spirit, and her God, should rise up against
the evil. And so it was. That is to say, despite
the long periods of suffering brought about as
much by the treatment as by the disease, and
despite the depression which fastened on her
from time to time—oh, too often!—she
maintained her dignity against the odds. She
laughed, she gave herself to her embroidery
and other pursuits, she remained interested
in the things of this world; and though she
couldn't help from time to time asking herself
why this had come to her, this curse, though
she even protested to God, she continually
returned to an equable state of mind,
accepting her struggle so long as she felt she

might live another day. No, it was not even that. So long as she could enjoy the day itself, the present day, she was more or less content.

Well, it was all over now, and she was lying here in the moonlight, the funeral long since over, and no one to grieve over her or distract her with anxieties they might cause her through making her feel she would like to help them but no longer could. She was enjoying the silence and the loneliness. She had always, in fact, been capable of enjoying her own company, even if she was gregarious too. But this peacefulness was better than any comparable experience of peacefulness she had had in life. And the other dead, what had become of them? Why did not one of them come to welcome her? No, the little field of tombstones remained absolutely silent, as though she were the only corpse there. Corpse? She was not a corpse. Could a corpse think, feel, as she thought and felt? Perhaps she was not dead, she thought with alarm. But no, no living person could have survived this burial, at any rate in the calm condition she was in; and then she remembered that she was not in fact breathing. Above her the bright stars shone and the gentle air moved through the branches of nearby trees and swept soothingly over the little mounds which included her own. She grew tired, like a child does, happily tired. She fell asleep.

Then came a dream, a nightmare rather. She was in the heavenly court indeed. The splendour overawed her, the sound of trumpets deafened her, her Judge sat in awesome majesty, a thousand angels were in attendance, there was a terrifying prosecutor whom she recognised at once as the Devil. His arguments were irrefutable, his contempt withering. Surely her case was lost. Then rose her defending counsel. Jesus surely! Oh, the trial went on for ages. Yes, it was not unlike that trial she had read about in the novel by Franz Kafka. It was just as bewildering. She was called to speak, to answer for herself; so, resolute as ever, she gathered the voluminous skirts of her magnificent dress about her and addressed the court. Her speech was banal in the extreme. The thoughts she had had on earth and which she was sometimes rather proud of reduced the prosecuting counsel to tears of laughter, and her defending counsel was clearly embarrassed. The Judge himself seemed to have fallen asleep. There was dead silence, except for the titterings of wayward angels and the open guffaws of Mr Satan. "Order! Order in court!" shouted the Judge, waking up suddenly, and banging his hammer. "Let the woman speak!" But poor Martha had collapsed in floods of tears. Though she had been able to withstand the taunts of naughty schoolchildren, this Satanic ridicule, and the reluctant complicity of the powers of Good itself, were too much for her.

"Well," said the Judge, "have you nothing more to say?"

"No," said Martha. "What's the good? No one is listening."

"Oh yes, we are," sneered Satan, "but you condemn yourself from your own lips."

"Enough!" cried the Judge. "I—"

But then Martha's dream dissolved. She was back in the grave, but no longer happy there. It was cold, damp, she was frightened, she could not breathe, she was dying again. She could not see the stars or feel the wind, she could not hear the occasional midnight sound. The worst pangs of her earthly disease seemed to have gripped her.

"No!" she called out, "no! God help me! God help me!"

There was a footstep. She heard a footstep. Someone was kneeling at the grave. She heard weeping, then a voice:

"Martha! Martha! Can you hear me? Can you hear me?"

But the voice broke down in sobs of heartbreaking intensity.

She wanted to soothe the speaker. She tried with all her strength to speak, to call up to him, "It's all right! It's all right!" but no sound came from her. This was an agony to her. Her greatest trial was now, in her inability to soothe the man—it was a man—who was so desperately calling to her. His sobs changed to a wail of utter sorrow. He began to tell her how much he loved her, wanted her, missed her; he would kill himself, he said.

"No!" she almost screamed with terror and anger. "You will not! You will not! Listen to me! Listen! Listen, you fool!"

But he could not hear her, and she knew it.

"Oh, God, God!" she prayed. "Save him! Save him!"

The weeping and the wailing and the sobbing went on.

Martha tried to bang on the sides of her coffin, and on the lid; and still she exhorted him to stop, to go home, not to be a fool, to live. But it seemed he would not listen. No, it wasn't that. He could not hear. It was death that separated them.

Whatever she did, the man outside, the man who lived, could hear nothing. But then it went quiet. At least it went quiet. What was going on, she wondered. Had he calmed down? Had he killed himself after all? No, he hadn't killed himself. He was whispering down into the coffin, whispering at the earth: "Martha," he was saying, "Martha, I'm sorry. Rest in peace, my love. Rest in peace."

Time

I bumped into him on Oxford Street! Yes, after all those years. How many? About fifty. You'll be surprised that I recognised him. After all, all I remembered was a scruffy teenage schoolboy, looking awed by the book he was reading in class. Yes, a text-book forsooth! It was Marlow. Well, that's what we called him. On account of the book he was reading. We were fortunate or unfortunate enough to have one of those Leavisite English Masters, and of course he was "doing" Conrad with us. I still don't know whether I should write "Marlow" or "Marlowe". Well, to tell the truth, I didn't recognise him; he recognised me. That's how it should be. People always mattered more to Marlow than Marlow mattered to them. That's how he was. I suppose that's why he was so interested in Literature, a subject I didn't much care for. But I rather liked Marlow nevertheless; and certainly our Leavisite teacher was a good one. He got us all more or less interested in the Conradian tale, though I'm afraid I've forgotten which one it was by now. Trouble was, the language was so damned difficult. No need for it. The whole thing could have been told with a much more reduced vocabulary and simpler syntax. And I don't believe the fact that the author was a foreigner was the reason. No, it was just pretentiousness. Foreigners have difficulty learning foreign words. I should know, with my stammering Spanish.

Anyway, this hand caught my sleeve and those curiously nervous but sometimes very direct eyes were looking into mine and, quietly, my name was pronounced. It didn't take long to re-establish contact, and we were genuinely glad to meet. The next thing was to arrange a more extended meeting, for I was on my way to a business meeting then, and there was no question of my missing that for a pleasant chat with an old classmate. So we arranged to meet a couple of days later at a quiet café he gave me the address of, where we could, he said, have a cup of tea and talk without interruption for as long as we liked. He said he had something particular he wanted to tell me.

It turned out that Marlow lived in London, as I didn't; and that he had been trying to become an author. That's to say a published one. But he never had any luck. I suppose his work was just not good enough, or not what was selling at the moment. I'm sure I don't know. The writing and publishing trade is a mystery to me, though I know there are fortunes to be made in it.

Anyway, he'd given up by the time I met him, and that's why he wanted to talk to me so much. You see, whilst he had given up writing things down, out of sheer despair at not getting them published, the urge to tell stories or whatever hadn't left him. So all he could do was speak them, as it were. Find a willing listener and spout. Recipe for becoming a bore. I say the urge to tell stories but, as he explained it to me, it wasn't so much stories as . . . . Frankly I don't know what he was trying to say.

I met him as arranged, and, after a few polite exchanges, he got down to business. "You've heard of those children, haven't you," he said, "who were brought up by animals? Abandoned by their parents or just lost in the bush. Found by animals, like wolves or bears, and brought up as one of them? There are several well-attested cases. But I believe the children never survive in a human environment afterwards, or if they do they are permanently damaged."

At this point I began to believe the poor man was mad: for he began to giggle wildly. But he simmered down and, looking at me with enormous seriousness, asked me whether I liked the singing of Beniamino Gigli! I stared at him. "Gigli," he said. "You've heard of Gigli?" "Of course, I have," I snapped. "But—" "Well, what do you think of his singing?" Wearily I told him that the man was long since dead, and that we were living in a later age of operatic performance, and that, though Gigli was, had been, etc. etc. Well, he cut me short again. "Gigli was the greatest tenor who ever lived." "All right," I said. "So be it. I'm sure I don't know."

Marlow grew misty-eyed. "I heard a reissued opera, in which he starred, recently," he said. "Such rich, ringing tones. Such elasticity. How can he be dead? How can he?" And then, with what you might call corny promptitude, he quoted: "*Où sont les neiges d'antan?*"

I was both impatient and troubled for him; but I decided to treat him without kid gloves. "*Les neiges d'antan* have long since melted," I said. "They will not come again, but other snow will fall. Same with the beautiful ladies the poet also had in mind. We die, you know."

He moved his tongue over his dry lips and murmured: "Yes, I know."

"Well," I said, in a livelier tone, "what about those wild children?"

"Oh yes," he took me up, smilingly. "You know, they would have no sense of Time."

I confess this had not struck me before, but I didn't see it had any but an academic interest. And I wasn't sure he was right, anyway.

We were silent for a few moments. I wondered if this wasn't the end of the eccentric conversation. "I think I'd like another toasted teacake," he said. "Would you?" I love toasted teacakes, so I said yes, glad to escape the weird intricacies of his mind, to tell the truth.

As we sat munching our teacakes and drinking deliciously sweet tea—it was a good café, I hasten to add—he took up the subject again.

"It was not long ago that another of these children was discovered—" I didn't know whether he was making the thing up or whether he really had read a report of it, but he was clearly under way with his story and I had no mind to interrupt. "Only she wasn't a child. She was a woman of about sixty-five who had been found by tribesmen somewhere in the wilds of Ethiopia, when she was a child, and had been living with them ever since, entirely unknown to the 'civilised' world. She was the daughter, it turned out, of a white woman and an African, being born about the time of the Italian invasion of Abyssinia. It appears that the woman had abandoned her child, probably because of the disgrace, and that animals had nurtured it, just as in the case of Romulus and Remus and the many heroes and heroines of other stories found in myth and legend, and even works of anthropology." Well, Marlow didn't know how long the child had lived with animals—jackals, I believe he said they were (which sounds pretty unlikely to me: but there we are)—but it was able to adjust to human society, and lived, as I say, according to Marlow's tale, a long life, till quite recently, entirely unknown to "civilisation".

"And then she heard this voice." Marlow stopped dead and looked me straight in the eyes, with a sort of deadly earnestness. "This voice . . . ." His own voice trailed away into silence; and I'll swear I saw tears rising in his eyes. "You won't understand!" he exclaimed (I thought angrily). "No one ever understands! Oh, they say they do. Everyone says they do. I tell you, I have sat in a church and heard the priest or minister or whatever other shallow hypocrite you care to call such, heard him say blandly: 'We are all going to die. But, take heart, dear brothers and sisters in Christ, there is another life—WHEN WE CAN ALL START ALL OVER AGAIN!' Fool! And he thinks we'll get to the end of that one, and start that one again!"

"Oh, come on, Marlow. We're not all bloody Buddhists, you know," I felt bound to interpose.

"No, and nothing else either!" he shouted. "Nothing else either! Nothing! Nothing! We are absolutely nothing! Me included."

Naturally the other patrons of the café were beginning to stare. "Come on, Marlow, my dear friend. Another toasted teacake?"

Fortunately for me, for both of us, he burst out laughing. "Yes," he said, "but not too well done."

When I got back to the table he was not so cheerful. He was shaking his head and muttering something about not being able to get his message across. I asked him what message that was and whether he thought he was a prophet or something. He was subdued. "Just that we are going to die," he said. It sounded feeble.

"Tell me more about the wild woman," I said.

Marlow brightened up. He clearly enjoyed the "act of creation". He was away on the wings of his fiction again, if it was fiction. He told me it was fact.

"This woman," he went on, "she heard a voice. It was like this. Her people were gradually, of course, being brought in from the outside. Soon the whole world will be inside. All the same. All the same gadgetry. Same standards of hygiene. Same Macdonald's cuisine. You know. Well, of course, she was listening to the radio. Normally, they don't transmit grand opera to the remote villages; but somehow the old woman heard a recording of a 1934 performance of *Pagliacci*. Yes, with Beniamino Gigli in the leading role. What a voice! And then she heard it. Sailing out from the voices of the chorus came the pure, beautiful soprano voice of her mother. She knew it as well as if she had heard it only yesterday. Something took place in the depths of her complex human memory to trigger that recognition. It was her mother! She went wild with excitement. She demanded to be taken to Addis Ababa, to get more information. Nothing could stop her. She trekked for God knows how many miles. She rode on carts, at a snail's pace. She even found herself on a train for a time. Anyway she got there. She was at the broadcasting headquarters. She got through to the administrators. Her persistence was absolutely irresistible."

Marlow laughed a little hysterically. He was on the point of tears. "She couldn't," he whispered, "believe that her mother was dead."

I sat there, waiting for him to go on. "I suppose," I said finally, to bridge the awkward gap in his story, "I suppose she had no sense of time."

"None," he said, as though relating the most stupendous and awful fact. "None at all. They had thought her 'normal', but she wasn't. She didn't understand that the voice she had heard, a voice belonging to a young, healthy, perhaps quite beautiful woman, was no longer to be heard from the living body of anyone. It was simply a sound in the ether, as it were. A dead thing, too. Just as the body that had once contained it was dead."

"But was she?" I quickly returned. "Was she dead? She needn't have been, perhaps. How long ago was it?"

Marlow shook his head. "That's not the point," he said. "Time is the point. Even if she were not dead, she would have been a haggard old woman. Her daughter, perhaps, only less haggard than she. This isn't a story about family relationships. It's a story about Time."

"I don't understand it," he went on. "I just don't understand it. We're here. We speak to each other. We breathe. We eat. We drink. We are alive. But we will be dead. Some day we will be dead. I hope we don't die horrifically. Nothing too long drawn-out. But we have no control. Unless we think of suicide. You, my friend, you have red cheeks. You look well. You are making a lot of money, yes? Well, I am not. I am driven almost mad with thoughts of death and of my own unworthiness. It was a mistake for you to meet me after all these years. I am hardly more than a ghost myself. We had better say goodbye now."

He got up from the table and walked across the room without looking back. I could do nothing but stare dumbfounded. Just before he reached the door he turned. "God be with you!" he called across, and went out into the street. I have heard nothing from him since.

The Smell of Civilisation

Exe now lived only with the beasts. He was unfit to share the society of his fellow men. He stank. He could no longer control his excretory functions, so he urinated and defecated involuntarily. Yet he was an intelligent, even good-looking, man of fifty-five. What should he do? He lived with the beasts. He thought he should live in a pigsty; but it hadn't come to that yet. He lived in the woods, with his dog, who did not seem to take exception to his disgusting smell. His dog loved him still. He seemed even to like Exe's smell. At any rate, he looked into Exe's eyes and saw they were just the same—shining, kindly eyes (as were the eyes of the dog). The man and the dog loved each other.

It had come on, the incontinence, quite gently. Just a little urine spurted into his pants without warning. Nothing remarkable. Easy to clean up, with a wash and a change. But matters gradually worsened, till they reached the present pass.

With great embarrassment he had consulted physicians, but finally decided to let Nature take its course. The temporary relief of symptoms was over. He was on his own.

His family rebelled. They called in a psychiatrist, against Exe's will. But Exe was inexorable. He would not be treated. If his family loved him, they would stay with him, as he was, for better or worse. They left. Exe smiled. He would find out who were his friends now! Mick, his dog, stayed. Seemed to love him more than ever, in his isolation. The man laughed, patted his dog, and took him out for a walk.

Humanity avoided him. Children laughed. He could not buy a loaf or enter a café. Besides, he insisted on being accompanied everywhere by his dog. "Dogs not admitted!" was a frequent sign. The Social Services came round. The Police. He had to compromise. Having agreed to seek medical treatment, and making himself presentable (as best he could), he succeeded in getting officialdom to (unwittingly) give him enough time to escape. He went to Wales. Into the woods. Among the mountains. But he knew they would track him down. His time was limited.

"So," he thought, "it amounts to this. Civilisation depends on smell. Cleanliness is next to godliness, but God will accept my prayers, just as this dog loves me for the sake of my eyes."

He patted the dog, which wagged its tail.

But the rain came. Soon the wood was a morass of mud, fallen leaves, and broken twigs. The two creatures huddled in their leaking bivouac. Light failed and the darkness thickened about them, with the wind howling. Sometimes the moon emerged from a gap in the clouds but was quickly smothered again in the dense blanket of billowing shapes.

Exe remembered his former self—dapper, smiling, liked by his colleagues, loved by his wife. Vanity. He was better off as he was.

The dog crept closer to him. He patted it and stroked its head. The wind howled, the rain poured down, the bivouac leaked.

Man and dog fell asleep.

As the dawn gradually crept westward, it revealed the sodden countryside upon which the rain had ceased to fall.

Exe cleaned himself up and went in search of food, accompanied of course by Mick. There seemed to be nothing for a human being to eat but blackberries. Mick found a few mice. There was nothing for Exe to do but approach his fellow man and ask for assistance.

They rambled a long way from the wood, up and down steep hillsides, till eventually they came upon a village. But what was the good? This was the next thing to returning home; so the pair trudged back to their tent. On the way, Mick started a hare, and he succeeded in running it to ground. Exe was delighted but his dog was not prepared to share the meal. Before Exe could snatch it away from him, it was a mess of blood and guts—and Exe had a bitten hand. The dog was hungry too. But Exe did not chastise the dog, for who had ever trained him? A lucky aim with a heavy stick gained Exe his dinner in the form of a pigeon, which Mick nearly stole.

That night Exe slept soundly, having first gazed happily at the stars; but in the morning he found that he had soiled himself again. You could not enjoy life if your pants were filling with excrement. That was the terrible truth. The only way to avoid it was not to eat.

A new day dawned—a brilliant day, dewy, clear, silent but for birdsong and the gentle movement of the wind. It was good to be alive. After cleaning himself up —Exe had taken care to camp by a stream—he whistled for Mick who had gone off exploring, and the two of them went for a pleasant stroll. Exe studied the flora and fauna, and enjoyed the different prospects the landscape offered, but knew he would have to be content, thus, with "unimproved" Nature, for no functionary of the National Trust would admit him to the ingeniously laid-out grounds of a stately home. In fact, he was stinking again.

The stench given off by Exe was really too much, even for himself, and he thought of committing suicide. By this time they had reached their camp and Exe took off his trousers to wash them. He could use his belt, if need be, as a noose.

"Grab the bloody dog!" he heard, as he turned, with trousers dripping in his hand, to see a policeman struggling to wrap the madly barking head of Mick in a blanket, and another policeman running towards himself.

Soon he was in the grip of this Constable, who told him that he had a warrant to arrest him for his own good. But Exe begged leave, in view of his condition, to relieve himself first. Before the Constable could make up his mind to release the madman (as he thought him) Exe vented an enormous fart and followed it by a thorough evacuation of his bowels. For the first time since his indisposition had taken hold of him did he thoroughly enjoy these bodily functions.

"You fucking bastard!" yelled the policeman who had released him; but Exe was now racing for cover with Mick, who had also escaped, at his heels. The second officer hurled himself in a magnificent rugby tackle at Exe's flying legs; caught them and brought his man violently down. But Mick, in his bewilderment, turned and bit the policeman in the face. This was no longer a farce, but it gave Exe and his dog time to, themselves, escape, as the unharmed policeman ministered to his comrade. Exe knew, of course, that it would not be long before a posse of policemen were combing through the woods, and he would be charged with more than disturbing the peace. Mick would no doubt be shot.

As they lay on the ground, enjoying a breathless respite from the chase, a homeless couple, a young man and his "partner", having watched in hiding the recent drama, in urgent tones, invited Exe and his dog to their bit of a camp, to wash in a nearby stream and to eat some dry bread. So long as their guests were enemies of the Police and the State, they were welcome to what humble assistance the pair could provide.

And so, before capture, Exe and his dog had found true friends.

The Old Ladies

They were three old ladies in a private hotel, in the lounge, sipping tea. One had an ear trumpet, one had very thin hair, and one a great mop of silvery-blue hair like a halo. And they were all rather well-off. They spoke with a variety of cracked and hoarse voices, sometimes very loud, sometimes too soft, and they generally repeated things two or three times, because they were hard of hearing But they were not good friends. Yet they had to live together, with the other guests, in the private hotel, so they tried to make the best of it.

At the far end of the room, well away from where the old ladies sat, was a television-set which they loathed. *Ça ne leur disait rien!* They felt it was almost an insult. For hadn't they their own lives to lead? And hadn't they a rich store of memories? What did the world mean by imposing this vulgarity upon them? Even though they were almost at the limit of life, waiting to step over into death, when the angel should come to lead them, they had no need of an artificial world.

Their minds were full of the past; and the past, in fragments, kept breaking out through their lips—people, places, opinions, dreams. They fought old battles, re-lived old amours, but, when threatened by the present, the three old ladies joined ranks to defend the past, and all the divisions within the past itself were healed in order to confront the impertinent present.

Yet they were like cannibals. They lusted each for the death of the other: for then the ranks of the glorious survivors, being thinned, would be endowed with still more honour. And they braved circumstance to try and prove their worthiness. They took trips, independently, to different parts of the capital, in which city they lived, in order to demonstrate that they were still capable of managing their lives as they had done in their youth; and if any of their number should perchance fail to return from one of these perilous excursions, well, the Law of Evolution would endorse the survival of those who were fittest.

The young women who served them, as maids or waitresses in the hotel, looked upon the old ladies with awe as well as disgust. They could not bear to think that they, too, would grow old, become crotchety, perhaps eccentric, begin to lose control of their bodily functions; yet they admired the indomitability of these old women. In fact they were even rather afraid of them, even though they did snigger behind their backs. For the old ladies chivvied them mercilessly, and, because of their superior education perhaps and the sophistication of the social ethos in which they had spent their lives, they were generally more than a match for the cheek of any mere slip of an ignorant girl, probably of foreign origin too.

The old ladies sat on easy chairs, propped up with cushions, sometimes resting their heads on their hands which were blue-veined, bony, and shook slightly under the weight of those fragile skulls, their eyes watering as though with purposeless tears. In summer they wore loose dresses of thin material, sometimes supplemented with silk or cotton shawls, so that their garments seemed to flow from them like those of weary goddesses. And they watched haughtily the brittle world that pranked itself ridiculously before them. They trod upon deep-piled carpets, beneath sparkling chandeliers, their clothing faintly perfumed to keep their persons sweet. Whilst the hubbub of strange voices was like a sea in which their imaginations moved as terrible fish. Barely blinking they lay, perilously, within the depth of their bodies, as pike in deep waters.

"Well, they brought me my cup of tea at half-past six this morning. And there was no milk. What do you think—no milk! So I said to her, when I caught her in the corridor, 'Where's the milk then?'"

"I don't suppose they brought you any."

"Eh? Brought me any? Oh yes, they did. But I had to make them. I said, 'What about all those jugs of milk standing outside the bedroom doors—those that people have finished with? Can't you give me one of those?' I said—"

"They wouldn't do that. Oh no, they wouldn't do that."

"Wouldn't they! Wouldn't they, though! I told her. But she was so stupid. Ah, they're so stupid these days! Do you know what she said? 'I can't do that, ma'am, but I'll go and get you some from downstairs.' And she did too. By that time my tea was cold, stone cold, I say!"

Sister Cecilia

Sister Cecilia took the sick man's head in her arms and smiled. His head lolled to one side—though she supported it—and the mouth dropped open, saliva dribbling gently down. She dabbed it with a piece of tissue and looked quietly, lovingly, into the unsteady eyes that watered helplessly, and there, in the depths of them, was an answering smile. From where she was sitting, Sister Cecilia could see the foliage of a tree and a section of the hospital road, because one of the two ward-windows was open. For the rest, all was bright light diffused by frosted glass.

"Do you want to lie back on the pillow?" she whispered, bringing her face very close to his.

The closeness of her body reassured him, yet its vigour gave him a pang of envy. He felt her warm breath like a caress, and the fresh scent of her habit made him long for his freedom. His mouth, unnaturally still, moved slightly at one corner, letting a faint "Yes!" escape him; and, as she leaned over, he was painfully aware of her healthy body moving beneath the stiff nun's clothing that rustled busily.

She was a handsome woman, with blue eyes and a clear complexion, the bone-structure of her face seeming to match the boldness of her character. Her speech was lively in normal circumstances and she had a loud frank laugh. No wonder no man could forget that she was a daughter of Eve. Nor could she forget it herself, though she strove to do so. Her fate had been made hard by the loudness with which the flesh called to her: as loud as the call of God.

As a girl she had shared all the temptations the other girls had been subject to, and she had succumbed as often as they; only, it was in the strength of her regret, her penitence, that the clear spirit showed itself until, it seemed to her, another presence was calling her. Somehow she sensed the surpassing beauty of that which was not visible. She could imagine a beauty that was more radiant than any natural beauty, which is not to say she could "see " that beauty in her imagination—indeed she knew she would never see it, in this life—but the hints she had were enough to give her an absolute confidence in its existence. Those hints she found in the beauties of Nature such as were revealed to her in the rhapsodic verses of the Romantic poets, especially those of Wordsworth whose purity of soul (as she imagined it) proved to be the ideal medium for the transmission of such deep and holy truth. But, though he was a Christian, she felt sad at the thought that he had worshipped at an imperfect altar, rather as Dante was saddened by the thought of Virgil, whom he so much revered, having lived and died a pagan. Yet the poets, inspired as they undoubtedly were and, no doubt, sent by God to reveal to us His beauty, were as nothing compared to—or at least were certainly less than—the Apostles and the saints. Contemplating these, it was not the beauty of the natural world that one apprehended, no, not even in so far as that was a hint of something infinitely finer, but the unspeakable divine beauty of the human soul in its relation to God. In His image He made man.

And so the sick man she now nursed was an image of God. Nothing could distract her from that profound saving truth.

Sister Cecilia went off duty; then, in the evening, came on again. About midnight Sister Catherine came to relieve her. The patient was sleeping peacefully.

"Sh—sh!" Sister Cecilia snapped, when the other nun begged her to go and get a bite to eat. "He's a light sleeper!"

"Oh, I'm sorry!" whispered Sister Catherine, in genuine dismay.

"I'll be back soon," said Sister Cecilia.

"Oh, don't hurry," replied Sister Catherine. "I don't mind how long I stay."

Sister Cecilia made her way out of the building and out into the night, under the magnificent display of stars. As she glanced up at them she caught her breath in wonder.

Look at the stars! look, look up at the skies!
O look at all the fire-folk sitting in the air!

—lines from one of her favourite poets, the Jesuit Gerard Manley Hopkins, came to her mind.

She entered the other building and made her way to the refectory, being greeted by a sudden gush of warm air as she crossed the kitchen to enter the dining-area, that route being the only possible one at this time of night. She greeted some acquaintances with whom she stood queuing in front of the steaming hot-plates, presided over by a jolly woman who held the big spoons, then made her way, with a plate of food, to one of the communal tables. There she talked gaily about the day's affairs until a disturbing thought came into her mind. Why did she tell Sister Catherine that her patient was a light sleeper? He wasn't a light sleeper. Why was she irritated in fact by almost everything that the well-meaning Sister Catherine did? There was no reason. Despite all her service and her fine feelings about the stars, she was as fallible as ever. She was angry without reason; she lied; she despised in some sense one of God's creatures, nay, one of his very children, made in His image. Love her neighbour? No, she despised him!

Sister Cecilia put down her knife and fork. She bade a civil farewell to her friends, and, finding a lonely place in the quiet building, she fell on her knees and prayed, with tears running down her cheeks.

Simberg

A dirty concrete stairway led up to a shabby door, labelled "Simberg". Inside, the electric lighting played on worn leather-upholstered armchairs, a polished table, flowered curtains, and jazzy wallpaper. A middle-aged couple occupied the flat.

The woman, small and plump, wore knitted cardigans in comfortable colours, which set off her shiny short black hair. Her dark eyes flashed a welcome. Her husband was gaunt, sad-eyed, his skin yellow. He wore grey trousers that needed pressing, and a waistcoat. Wire-rimmed spectacles magnified his bulbous eyes. His thin hair lay over a bony head, which cocked curiously if you asked him a question. His hands looked normal.

He had a vast collection of gramophone records, pre-electric included. He sent for them all over the world—New York, Berlin, Salzburg. He knew every conductor and soloist by name; he could recognise their style of performance. He had decided opinions. Yet he balked at discussion. His manner was to grunt, knowingly, then mumble his own opinion. His career had been cut short by an accident. The guiders of his hands were smashed, so he could not play the piano.

His wife did not understand his passion for music, but she indulged him, letting him spend beyond his means upon it, without complaint.

Now he worked in a clothing factory, packing suits for postal despatch, earning very little. But he was not unhappy. He enjoyed the mechanical activity and the idle conversation of the women who worked with him, though his contribution was a series of inexplicable exclamations—naive surprise or cryptic animosities. They, too, were indulgent to him.

Then one day he met a real musician. She had come with her mother who was an old friend of the family. With the ardent spirit of a girl she questioned the laconic maestro. She could go further than other people, take greater liberties on account of the common Euterpian blood. She could coerce his mind along forgotten paths, drive him back into his youth, recover the ghost of his since splintered personality. He winced but endured the ordeal.

The problem was to distinguish between what was dream and what reality. He made reference to past luminaries, like faded petals falling: Harold Samuel, Busoni, Artur Schnabel, Alfred Cortot. He had studied music in Paris, lived in Montmartre. The family had been rich. The colour of his past enriched the present of his interlocutor. A proud smile accompanied the toss of triumph to which such unembittered memories forced his head. It was the treasured possession no catastrophe could ruin. To the actual disaster he seemed blind. The girl marvelled as he spoke of the period between the wars, before "universal indifference" to the arts had set in, prior to the ultimate victory of Technology, when Art was still a power. The desert of a Philistine present stretched before the pained vision of his guest, who knew for the first time the real cause of Simberg's complacency.

Did lost years always appear brighter than those present or was it people alone who made them bright?

Simberg shuffled in his dusty collection of gramophone records, emerging finally with a recent acquisition.

"This record," he said, "you have not heard. Beethoven's Sixth Piano Concerto."

He never offered explanations. He liked to play with the curiosity of his listeners. It was a trying business getting him to hand over the facts; he hoarded them like gold bars. It was the last vestige of his artist's power.

"Sixth Piano Concerto. That's what I said. From America. Yes, Beethoven. I said Beethoven. I've got the music too. No, never. Never lend it to anyone. Never out of my sight. You don't believe me? Well, listen."

He put the rare piece on the turntable.

"You didn't *know* Beethoven made a transcription of his Violin Concerto, for piano?" said Simberg, with his queer emphasis.

The music rang through the comfortable but inglorious room, thrilling the souls of the two musicians, one who had lived and one living, Simberg enjoying the astonishment his discovery had caused. It was his only hold on a world from which he had been cruelly barred. Plangent melodies rose from the electronic box, a box more priceless than a casket of jewels. The debutante spiritually knelt before its mean presence, her eyes lit with enthusiasm, with deep admiration. Simberg's spectacles glittered with satisfaction. In the grate a good fire licked its way into the darkness of the flue, as though symbolising the intensity of artistic inspiration burning triumphantly through the darkness of the soul.

Suddenly the fingers of the crippled pianist began to twitch uncontrollably and his protégée stared in fascination. She could imagine them racing down the keyboard in arpeggios and hammering out the richly plotted chords. An orchestral climax shook her heart with insuppressible emotion and filled the bright eyes with still brighter tears.

Jackdaw

I don't myself know how to play bridge, but Jackie played it skilfully. She built her life round it. Round that and drink and cigarettes. Well, that's an exaggeration, of course. Who would admit to his life being based on that? There were, of course, "human relationships". It makes us feel better to think our lives are based on "human relationships". It makes us feel human! She was a widow. Once she had been more or less happily married, but that was many many years ago. Since then she had been "on her own". She lived alone and she played cards several times a week.

The house was a modest semi-detached situated in a middle-class area of a large provincial town. Jackie kept it neat, for that's how she had been brought up, and how all her friends had been brought up. It was expected. She was not well-off but she managed to seem better-off than she was. Trouble was, too much went out on whisky.

She was a small, dark-haired person, with sharp features. Once she had been decidedly good-looking, though always with a somewhat affected air that put people off. It didn't put Gerald off though, nearly forty years ago. He was a quiet-spoken, small, neat man, who always contrived to leave the impression that he was hiding something. Not anything discreditable, but a "depth". They made a good couple, quietly going about their business, with an air of secrecy about them, as though hiding a life others might criticise.

But there was nothing to tell about them. No scandal. Nothing.

Jackie's father had been a provocative man. Short-statured, rather fat, aggressive in manner. You didn't meddle with Morris Coe. Her mother, too, had been a decidedly self-confident woman, with a touch of arrogance even; so it wasn't surprising that Jackie should turn out a bit "difficult" too. But whereas her parents had made their way in the world, had a secure place in it, Jackie seemed somehow on the fringes of things. Perhaps it would have been different if she had had children, but she and Gerald were not blessed with a family of their own.

Years slipped by, as they always do, imperceptibly. People doing the same things, talking to the same people, breathing the same air. In a way, not changing. It is Time only that changes, washing over people without their noticing— the tide of Time.

Eventually their clothes wore out, or they grew tired of them. So they acquired others. They could afford it. But it was the same "them" inside. People don't change, though they may think they do. They think, usually, that they have grown wiser, more "mature". It's rubbish, self-flattering rubbish, usually.

"You little Austrian! You little Austrian!" That's how Mrs Coe used to go on when her husband annoyed her; for indeed he had been born an Austrian-Pole. And his arrogance she put down—or pretended to—to that. But he blazed at her just the same. And poor Jackie—Jacqueline, as she was to her socially-conscious mother—looked on with dismay, and often tears. Nevertheless, she inherited, as people often do, some of the same qualities that caused her to suffer so much as a child.

Had Jackie and Gerald had children it might have been different; they might have changed. Or rather, if not changed, then watched, and watched over, the change in their children; for indeed the child changes into an adult. And this involvement with other lives might have amounted to a sort of change in themselves. For that would have been a form of love, and love forces the mind outside itself. They would have been themselves but without their characteristic self-absorption. They would have been nicer people, perhaps. As it was, it wasn't children that concerned them, but cards—cards and clothes, cigarettes, and, sometimes only, whisky.

But they had their circle of friends, people much like themselves, only people with children mostly, and with their own circles of other relationships. All these people were spending their holidays from Death in a big provincial English town— eating, drinking, talking, loving, etc. Death happened now and then, usually to the previous generation. They were shocked; they wept; they tried to forget it.

They had an outing, once or twice a year, to the cemetery, where their fathers and mothers, and aunts and uncles, poor Marjory who died at eighteen, and little Peter, lay silently in the earth, with little pebbles or slabs of stone on top, to stop them rising out of their coffins perhaps. The minister had said prayers over their corpses as they were lowered into the grave, and the relatives stood round out of respect. But why should a corpse be respected by virtue of being one, when the living entity was perhaps unworthy of it?

Nevertheless, the officious mourners would leave their "dear ones" in peace eventually, and the dead would have the cemetery to themselves again.

All the birds of the air, the very worms, the grass, and the trees eventually, would die. Everything would be renewed and the dead would be as if they had never been. Even Jackie. Even Gerald.

Mr and Mrs Morris Coe were already gone.

But the children would go on for a while; and then they too would be gone.

Jackie sometimes thought of these things. Most of her friends, and Gerald certainly, pushed the thoughts aside, if they should occur. It was enough to have to visit the cemetery now and then.

They all watched television of course, and saw films, or even read books; and death was cropping up all the time there. But there it was entertainment or information, not something real. Even when the media-people stressed how tragic things were for some people, it didn't really go home to most of their audience, no, not even if it made them dig deep for a charitable donation. It was, Give and Forget, for you at any rate had not ignored the beggar's bowl. But the only answer to the call was actually to (in Christian idiom) take up the Cross, give all to the poor. And even then, you mightn't glory in your action, for that would be to ruin every chance of salvation you might have, even if the poor might still be served.

Jackie revolved these thoughts but she didn't bestir herself. She had no thought of being a martyr. Not at all. She would rather contemplate her own unworthiness. It just made her think how awful people were, herself included.

So she began to have recourse to the bottle, to forget, to make herself happy. And the treatment worked wonders. She was happy; she did forget. Only the spectacle of his wife's inebriation struck terror into Gerald. He knew whither it must lead, as did Jackie of course. But why save herself? What for? For Gerald? No, she didn't love him enough for that. But no one else knew yet about her compulsion which was not yet an addiction.

But there was a marked improvement in her attitude on social occasions, such as card-playing. She seemed more positive, a little more extrovert, capable of a witty sally now and again. She was better, too, at cards. In fact she became a formidable gambler. She and Gerald took a Riviera holiday on the proceeds.

At first she enjoyed herself, strolling along the Promenade des Anglais, eating "bouillabaisse", drinking red wine, then a "digestif" and a coffee. She and Gerald turned brown through long hours on the sunny beach. But the dread of death encroached even here. Only oblivion could save her from despair, and this she could have quickly with the aid of strong spirit.

It didn't matter if she was drunk in Nice, because no one she knew was there. But she was mistaken to think no one there knew her. Nice is too popular a resort for anyone to feel safe from friends or acquaintances in, and though he did not intrude on the couple an elderly man who had known Jackie's father watched her one day from the other side of a hotel lounge.

But the sun still shone, the sky was blue, the pebbly beach hot and crammed with people doing what people do—laughing, talking, breathing, changing their positions, getting up, walking about, swimming, buying an ice-cream, etc., etc., etc. It was a lovely way to spend time; so long as you didn't think about death. But Jackie couldn't stop herself thinking about death, unless she was drunk. So she drank, and drank, and drank.

The effect on Gerald was what you might imagine. He was distraught. He was not enjoying his holiday, even if Jackie was enjoying hers, which she was—when she was drunk. So why be sober? Why, why be sober? For Gerald's sake? Phooey. Let Gerald look after himself. He had the better of it anyway. He wasn't obsessed by death.

Jackie began to feel vindictive towards him, precisely because he was so much better off than she. He was not obsessed by death. She knew, of course, that she was. She wasn't a fool. Far from it. But then she was right. Death was inevitable and it did make a nonsense of everything, just everything, a person did. So let's forget. Let's drink, drink, drink, and to hell with everyone and everything. Jackie was insufferable.

Of course, people began to notice now. You couldn't miss her, coming in to dinner with a silly supercilious grin on her sharp-featured face, staggering slightly, knocking over her wine-glass.

Happy? She wasn't happy, but she was drunk, and that was better than being sober, which was the normal condition of consciousness, consciousness that was insufferable to a person like her.

But Nice was a city which boasted an excellent casino. Let's go gambling. She watched the roulette ball whizz round a few times, but that was a nonsense too. There was no skill involved, just luck. Well, she didn't think of herself as favoured by Lady Luck, so let's play cards.

But here was some competition. There were professional gamblers here, with card-I.Q.'s of a very high level. She enjoyed the challenge. She lost some and she won some. Jackie, too, was respected now. It didn't matter if she got drunk— she didn't play when she was actually drunk (though what she had in fact drunk would, by this stage of her alcoholic career, have made most people incapable)—the fraternity cared only about her skill, or luck (for much still depended on what cards Fate dealt you), and her alcoholic excesses were considered, if anything, an addition to her charms. Here, surely, in Nice, at the Casino, was her true setting.

Gerald looked on helplessly. The couple quarrelled, but he was hopelessly outmatched by her. He was a mild man, without much capacity for temper. He merely suffered.

But all good things come to an end. The holiday was about to terminate. They had a 'plane to catch. They must pack. There were bills to pay. Thank God! (thought Gerald); for Jackie did consent to leave. On balance, she hadn't done all that well, anyhow. The competition had been stimulating, but a little overpowering.

So back they went to England, through the blue air, high above the clouds, in the sealed tube that was the aeroplane, high above the snow-capped mountains and the misty plains, the green valleys, the tiny-seeming towns, the winding ribbons of rivers, the straight roads. But Jackie didn't see much after the tray of drinks came round, for she kept re-ordering, of course.

Once back they resumed their previous pattern of life, and amazingly Jackie managed to keep her alcoholism secret from all but her very closest friends, whose loyalty was unimpeachable. Certainly she was seen to indulge herself with a glass or two during games of bridge, or at other social gatherings, but she was never caught with her guard down. Only when people 'phoned her at odd hours, and Gerald was not there to answer the call, would the caller hear a strange tone in Jackie's voice, and some strange thoughts from her lips; but she had always been a slightly unusual person, so the caller would let it slide. Now and again Jackie would tell a caller that she had taken a sleeping tablet, which might account for her slurred speech, for it was known that, like her mother before her, she suffered with her "nerves".

But things went from bad to worse. Once, she set the bedclothes alight, falling asleep with a cigarette between her fingers. Gerald didn't sleep with her any more. The result was a visit to the hospital out-patients department, where she was treated for burns. It didn't take the duty doctor very long to decide that she had been under the influence of alcohol, but Gerald maintained that it had been her birthday and that they had both had a drop too much. The doctor said nothing.

And now Gerald himself began to get ill. He had never been a robust man, and what with the worry about Jackie and her neglecting him, which is what she virtually did, and the seeming impossibility of getting her to seek professional help, well, he began to weaken, his system began to give way. He suffered from stomach pains; he had headaches; he began to grow breathless after very little physical activity.

This manifest deterioration in the physical condition of the man she had married, the man she had once cared for and loved, at last began to make an impression on the poor woman. She didn't after all want to lose him; and she could no longer claim that her condition was necessarily worse than his. Pity for him began to grow in her hardened heart. But it was too late. One day a policeman arrived to tell her that Gerald had had an accident in his car. It seemed that he had had a heart-attack and lost control. He was dead before the car collided with a bus.

With the house empty day and night, Jackie began to lose track of time. There was no pattern to her life. Only the daylight and darkness divided Time, and, when she could close curtains and switch on the light, she could ignore those indications too. The clocks might read a.m. or p.m., it made no difference to her.

Of course her few friends tried to help, but she made things difficult for them. She became aggressive, like her father had been; and arrogant, like her mother. She assumed a silly supercilious voice more and more often;

and she went on drinking. She did not play cards any more; she barely left the house—which was no longer tidy but neglected. She ate what she could lay her hands on. Occasionally she would go out and visit a supermarket where she would stock up for a month, filling her trolley with bottles of whisky as well as with tins of food. But she could not pay her bills. The cheques bounced; the cash-card was withdrawn.

But Jackie was not without relatives, and they tried to rally round her. They managed to pay off her debts; and even found a fairly substantial investment which, in her irresponsible state, Jackie, despite her erstwhile cleverness, had forgotten about. At least financially the household could be kept going. But where was the final answer to be found? She would not hear of consulting Alcoholics Anonymous. She didn't even recognise her condition. She thought she could "reform" whenever she wanted to, but she never wanted. After all, life was so good under the influence of alcohol that the poor compensations of sobriety, in the form of neat shelves, clean clothing, banal talk, regular hours, meant nothing to her. She didn't care for society, she didn't care for a new relationship with a man—or a woman.

Only one person in the world she cared for, and that was her cousin Sheila. She had always been close to Sheila and now Sheila was the only person in the world she cared for.

They would sit for long hours together, reminiscing, discussing where Jackie had "gone wrong", for she, as it were, played with the idea of having gone wrong, in the confidential intimacy of Sheila's company; but Sheila had a husband and children. Even Sheila found Jackie impossible. Nevertheless, she had patience with her, and she in fact still loved her. And Sheila was the one reality which gave Jackie pause, gave her some reason to go on living—well, Sheila and whisky itself. For Sheila somehow was inside her, inside Jackie: she was in a way a part of herself, the part that didn't want to give up, the part that clung to the everyday banality of things. So, living with herself, for Jackie, was a bit like the experience of Jacob wrestling with the angel. She had an entity within her from which she could not get free, so as to fulfil her own destiny, which was self-destruction. She must struggle and struggle, and yet she would be thrown down and go on living. And this without any great effort on Sheila's part, only the resilience of her love.

Yet it wasn't enough. One day the neighbours noticed that her lights were still on during the daytime, and though she was known to keep strange hours, a particular busybody 'phoned the police. They broke in and found Jackie unconscious. She had taken an overdose of sleeping tablets.

When she came to, in hospital, she maintained that it had been an accident. She told them that she had been drunk. After all, it was a free country. She could get drunk if she liked. Soon she was haranguing the staff embarrassingly, and they had to leave things be. Sheila almost gave up on her, but she was her cousin and only friend. And she loved her.

Then Sheila became ill. Several weeks after Jackie had been discharged from hospital, Sheila was diagnosed as suffering from an incurable cancer. Jackie watched her diminish and suffer and finally die, leaving a heart-broken husband and young family. Jackie knew now that life was a vicious snare. She did not believe in a God, so she had nothing to rail at but life itself—the sheer manifestation of life: the air, the clouds, the grass, the buildings, the people, the creatures, the noise, the movement, her very self. She retired to bed with her "comfort" —two bottles of Scotch.

And she drank steadily. She put the television on. She dozed. She drank. She staggered downstairs and made herself a sandwich. Then she went to bed again and drank. Her light was on all through the night. She was ill. She swallowed tablets. She revived. She drank. She 'phoned another cousin, someone else who had been concerned about her but who had been rebuffed too often to feel free to intrude. Would Vron get her a bottle of whisky? She felt ill and she knew that only that would help. Veronica protested but gave way, Jackie sounded so terribly and heart-brokenly persuasive. She promised to come round within the hour.

Jackie sank down into the bedclothes. She smiled because relief was at hand. But she laughed too, to think she could so beguile someone. Then she wept. Then she drifted off into an uneasy doze.

And she dreamed. She dreamed she was flying home from Nice, with Gerald at her side, only she wasn't drinking the time away, she was talking with him affably; she heard herself laugh—a gentle, friendly laugh; and he laughed too. She was gazing out of the window, marvelling at the beauty of the snow-capped mountains, the misty plains, the winding rivers, the straight roads. She was enjoying the flight as she had never, in life, enjoyed perhaps anything. "So," she thought, "it did not pass me by. I knew. I knew how wonderful things were. I knew how lovely life was. Only I couldn't break through to it."

The 'plane seemed to give a lurch. She knew it would crash. But she did not panic.

Alone of all the passengers, who were screaming and clutching each other as the 'plane dived through the air, she sat there, with a little smile on her face. Only she was not, by this time, actually sitting. No, the 'plane twisted in the air and turned upside-down and people were screaming or had lost consciousness as their bodies were wrenched by the straps that held them to their seats. But Jackie had not fastened her seat belt. She was somehow suspended in the air, not whirled off balance but stable there, like a bird.

She heard someone knocking at the door. It was Vron with the bottle. "Thank God!" she murmured. But she could not get down to open the door. So she tried to shout, but hardly a sound escaped her. Veronica panicked. She went next door and asked if anyone could help her get in the house. But they were an elderly couple, so, once again, the police were called. They knew where to come without difficulty this time.

Jackie was in the hospital again, and stayed there for two weeks. Her relatives were told that she must not be left alone. They could not answer for the consequences. There was a family conference. Could Jackie be forced to have treatment? Had they the authority to invoke such a drastic measure? She was due out of the hospital in a day or two.

Something had to be done. But it wasn't as though anyone could prove she had tried to commit suicide. In fact, that possibility had been ruled out. No, she was simply a woman who could not be trusted to go on living like other people did, and who, as a consequence, might end up doing away with herself either accidentally or on purpose. But it was her life.

What would her aggressive little father have said, and her arrogant mother? They would have cursed her and cajoled her, and dominated her, as they always had done; but there was no one left to guide her now, even by as rough means as these. Poor Gerald would have been able to do nothing but look on helplessly, as he always had.

She was a fierce bird was Jackie, and no one could get the better of her. But neither could she get the better of herself. Her nature was to swoop on carrion and be sick on it. Once she had been young, with dark eyes and dark hair, a slender nose and narrow face, a trim figure, a knowing sideways look. She had cast a spell upon Gerald. Hopelessly he had fallen in love with her, and for a time their marriage was a good one; but then the dissatisfaction set in, the obsession with death and decay. Where had it come from? Out of the heart of life itself, surely. Only a fool failed to see that even the sun must die.

She could not live in a world of illusion. She had wanted to shout at her fellow men and women, to remind them that death was waiting for them, that they were all simply on holiday, a short holiday, the holiday from death that life is. They were all at the Casino in Nice waiting for the roulette-wheel to spell out their fate. It was funny really, that people should be such babies, not to recognise what a world they were living in. Only those who could cast their thoughts outside themselves, to their children perhaps, could survive without being disgraced by their ignorance.

She returned home. Nothing had been done. She succeeded in repelling all would-be help. She went back to the bottle. The same disastrous routine was re-established, even to the sudden emergency calls for help and the occasional hospital detentions. Time slipped on as it will. Nothing was changed. People don't change. Only Time itself seems to change, and the change in the body from childhood to maturity, with its small change of personality perhaps.

Dementia began to set in. She imagined herself a bird, a jackdaw. Sometimes she was suspended near the roof of the body of that 'plane, watching the passengers plunge to their deaths screaming, clutching each other, but helpless; sometimes she was free in the outside air, floating over the snow-capped mountains where no bird could ever fly; sometimes she sat on the fence in her own back garden, watching Mrs Gregory hang out the washing, or children play in the garden of the house beyond; sometimes she grabbed bits of bacon-rind that someone had thrown for her. Once she sat on a man's outstretched arm, just to observe his incredulity at being visited so unexpectedly from Wild Nature, as it were. She laughed inside herself.

Now indeed she had entered the world of illusion, in a way she had not bargained for. And now there was reason to force her to have treatment. She was detained in a hospital where such cases as hers are treated, if not cured. But it didn't matter to her. She was a jackdaw now, free to roam the skies. Nothing could upset her any more. Everything was simply part of the free life she had attained at last. She needed no stimulant. She needed no human "relationship". And she died happy.

Ashkenazi

She came from Gevatayim but she went to live in Shekhunat-Hatikva. She had not come down in the world but gone up, gone up on the wings of idealism. She was a German Jewess living in Israel, who had determined to do something about the growing racialism of Oriental Jew against Western Jew and Western Jew against Oriental. The situation was insufferable, she thought, for Jews. Soon there would be a National Socialist movement, with a policy of regrouping the Orientals in another country. Wasn't there already a scheme on foot to concentrate them in the scalding Negev? Concentration camp of the Negev! Horror!

But she wasn't a very strong woman—in fact rather frail and world-weary. Yet her gentle eyes shone with a tender radiance that melted opposition and silenced criticism. She was a "gutinke". The neighbours looked pityingly on her as she packed her bags and gave orders to the burly removal men to manipulate her trunks into the vast hollows of the waiting pantechnicon. Her voice was quiet but they seemed to take notice and in the belongings went, like victuals into the maw of a metal monster. It was rather horrible to see, the inevitability of it. It seemed almost as if Geveret Salomon's very life were being swallowed up, yet she observed it herself with composure.

Then the vehicle moved off through the busy Tel Aviv streets, Geveret Salomon following in a taxi. The van rattled past apartment blocks gleaming white in the sunlight, animated café terraces, crowds of shoppers: stopping and starting at the lights, an item in the flow of traffic, with the blue sea flowing more quietly towards sandy beaches.

They came to Shekhunat-Hatikva, no longer happy. It was run-down, shabby: a curious sense of tragedy hung over all, despite the loquacious *leben*-sippers and squealing kids. The dark skins seemed to exude some malevolent mystery, as though of souls who inhabited a sinister kingdom. And the women stared stonily as the foreign lady opened her door to admit the removal men with her clean, good-quality goods. But their eyes shifted immediately their new neighbour turned to smile, yet pierced to the very quick of her flesh when she turned away. Despite herself, Geveret Salomon was relieved to shut the door on them.

She had two dark rooms downstairs and a shabby bedroom above. The staircase was rickety in the extreme and plaster peeled off the greasy walls. Geveret Salomon would change all that. For the present she must

begin at the beginning; so, after unpacking
only a few necessaries, down on her knees
she fell and scrubbed at the muddy, rat-
streaked floor. She would get one place into
shining respectability, then invite the strange
women who, she imagined, were uncannily
still clustered round her front door. Curious
how terrified the bursts of wild laughter,
from above and around, made her. Surely, only
other occupants of the gloomy apartment
block—for she had not the whole building to
herself—or friendly merriment outside?
Nevertheless, she was nervous. There might
be difficulties of course, but were they not all
Jews? All of one blood? What had centuries
of separation to do with it? Didn't we all say
"Next year in Jerusalem!" whether fair or
dark, English or North African, German or
Persian, French or Yemeni, American or
Turkish, Chinaman or Cochin Indian? So, the
gentle lady scrubbed with even greater force.

Next day she woke early, put on her usual
simple dress, and went out to buy provisions.
The street was in heavy shadow, for the sun
had not yet got above the tall blocks, nor
penetrated the narrow aperture of blue sky
between. It was cold but full of promise for
when the sun should make his entrance.
Geveret Salomon hummed to herself as she
strode down the street, smiling at the
shawled women on either side. Some smiled

back this time, though still guardedly, or else
with insincere expansiveness. A little band of
children followed her at heels, like a company
of mischievous elves. She gave them sweets
and they took hold of her skirts. The dark
women called them back in harsh-sounding
Arabic. Strange how the Eastern language
grated on Western nerves, so insensitive it
seemed, prickly as desert shrubs, dry as sand,
yet guttural with the gutturalness of parched
throats, alien almost as Chinese. But the
children took no notice, their bright eyes
begging for further gifts.

Geveret Salomon reached the corner
which opened on a main street busy with
traffic. But she had determined to do her
shopping amongst the Oriental Jews, so she
crossed over to where her new district
reasserted itself after the division wrought
by the highway. She entered a dingy store
presided over by a bearded Moroccan, who
instantly ushered her to the counter. "What
did the Geveret want? Surely he had in stock
everything she could desire! Wouldn't she
care to savour some Oriental cooking spices?
He would see she were not overcharged. Oh,
how many unscrupulous shopkeepers there
were in Tel Aviv! And how awful it was,
their all being Jews!" The obsequiousness
shocked her, but the little lady steeled
herself to the trial she knew must frame her

new life. For it was a new life. She was not
going to turn her back on it, no matter what
difficulties lay ahead. You could not run a
country on a basis of separate citizenship.
There must be only one community. Of
course, that community must be Western in
character, for the Western peoples were in
the cultural ascendant. There would be no
State of Israel without them. The great
Zionists had all come from the West—
Germany and Russia. Wasn't Hertzl himself
an Ashkenazi?

Yet on her way back to her new home,
Sarah Salomon turned off on the highway, to
sit at a little European café, where they sold
Viennese coffee and ice cream. It was a relief
to put down her heavy bags and sit in the
shade of a gaily coloured parasol, listening to
German being spoken and looking at the
glinting traffic as it sped by. She knew that it
was traitorous of her to do so, but she
basked in the sunshine of familiarity and
dreaded the moment when she must leave.
For the first time, she said to herself that
turning the corner fifty yards away was
entering a different country. It was hardly less
a contrast than sailing from Marseilles to
Rabat.

That evening she expected her first
visitors, the family of Iraqis from upstairs.
She had prepared a simple dinner, nothing

sumptuously off-putting: just a few potatoes, some mutton and a fancy pudding to follow. There was a bottle of orange juice and a bottle of ordinary red wine on the white tablecloth set for four—herself, the husband and wife, and the husband's elderly mother. At eight o'clock a timid knock announced her visitors. Sarah Salomon fled to the door and opened it, with a beaming face. The three guests merely stood there, sheepishly.

"Come in!" cried the German lady.

And in the Iraqis came.

It was not an unsatisfactory occasion. The ice was soon broken and the four people conversed in amicable Hebrew. Sarah learnt how the family Chelebi had owned a small carpet-making business in Kerbela; they made the carpets at home. The old lady's husband had been beadle of a local synagogue, but had died some fifteen years ago, before his family emigrated. Life had always been a struggle in Kerbela, till eventually the little carpet business quite failed, and the Chelebis were only too glad to leave the country and start a new life abroad. But, frankly, they had been surprised, on coming to Israel, to find a land so unlike their own, so unlike what they had pictured from the Bible, so European! They felt like fish out of water. They were told what to do, where to go—were in fact thoroughly organised. It both pleased and offended them. But to land up where they now were! That was an insult, wasn't it? The mean house, the dirty neighbourhood. They had seen where the Europeans lived. Why could they not live where the Europeans lived? Because the Europeans were in control. But they wouldn't always be—the little man became quite excited, his eyes gleamed. The Europeans would soon be outnumbered! Then the Orientals would vote for their own leaders, and their own leaders would rule Israel!

It was the wine had made him so voluble.

Sarah Salomon was, at this moment, chagrined. The situation seemed hopeless, her worst fears realised. But she, at any rate, was on the spot, could do something. So she tried to counter the little man's arguments. But he grew contemptuous, even abusive. What did she know? Merely a woman!

Merely a woman! Sarah's blood boiled. A woman! A woman! Was she not as good as any man? What did the little fool mean by slighting her womanhood? Did he think of her as so much in chattels, like an Arab woman? What did his own womenfolk think?

To her horror and amazement, she found they deferred to him. They said Moses made it quite clear that woman was inferior to man. At any rate, so distinct was her function that it was presumptious of her to meddle with politics. Her place was in the home.

Nevertheless, Sarah kept her temper as best she could. She changed the subject, thinking that only by slow, patient effort could the two worlds be made to meet—or rather, could the Eastern world be made to meet the Western. Her gaze fell upon the old lady. How utterly abhorrent she was, really. So fat and unmannerly. It wasn't merely her age. She refused to be polite because she enjoyed the kind of sneer associating with dirt enabled her to level at the world. That was it: these people wanted to sneer the underdog sneer at everything! She could see it in the eyes of the little man as he warmed to the alcohol and gabbled politics. But perhaps his wife was different. At any rate, she was the only one of the three who deigned to call her by her proper name. To the others, she was merely "Ashkenazi".

This appellation, "Ashkenazi", was adopted by the whole neighbourhood. "Where are you going, Ashkenazi?" the slovenly women would jeer. "Haven't you found a husband yet, Ashkenazi? You can't have ours!" They would become quite gross. It was as if they didn't think of her as a woman at all. They could insult her as much as they liked because, not only was she not an Oriental, she was not even a woman to them. And she belonged to the community which had landed them all in the squalor of Tel Aviv. But never mind. Just wait. Soon the Orientals would outvote the Westerners. Soon the plush hotels would be full of dark-skinned Jews from the East. Real Jews!

And the most Orthodox Israelis connived at the Oriental prejudice. They, too, hated the secular development of the state. They advanced reactionary ideas of government with the support of the backward Orientals. They grew more and more powerful, till the only answer to their threat was to curtail their democratic privileges. At least, that's how the picture looked in the dark future, unless universal secular education could break down the barriers. For the present, German and Iraqi stood in mutual enmity.

Yet Sarah hoped, by realising the problem, somehow to solve it, though, after two months, she began to think it impossible to conciliate her neighbours. It appeared that only to be like them—not merely tolerant of them—would pacify them. And that she couldn't be. They must reach her standards, not she descend to theirs. So the struggle went on, till she became a figure of fun even to the children. Only the Chelebis maintained reasonable relations, though the husband spoke behind her back and the old woman schemed to have her evicted from the property, as a corrupting influence.

But the younger woman showed some sympathy for the German lady. She visited her occasionally, when her husband was out and the old woman asleep. These meetings were strange little confabulations: an exchange of culinary information, with tentative gropings after an area of common understanding. Shulamith was a beautiful woman, whose darkness suggested warmth and intimacy, her eyes quiet and lustrous. But the more she saw of Sarah, the less she cleaved to her arrogant Iraqi husband and the more she shrank from her coarse-mannered mother-in-law. Their association in fact seemed to pre-figure the solution to the present-day actuality: the Orientals would become more "enlightened" and the Westerners learn some bits of exotic cooking. A strangely disproportionate bargain.

Sarah could not stay in Shekhunat-Hatikva, despite her good intentions. The discomfort was too much for her—the squalor and animosity. She must seek out her own kind, but without recriminations. There must be no racial intolerance on her side, regardless of what might come from the other or from her own people. So, one fine day, the removal van called again, and deposited her belongings where they really belonged.

Boche

Marianne fell in love with a German officer, in Bélignan, in the time of the Vichy administration. One day he came into the shop whilst she was stacking groceries on a high shelf, standing on a ladder. She was suspicious of this "foreign conqueror" but flattered by his courteous salutation. Slowly she descended the ladder, refusing the unnecessary proffer of a helping hand. He was struck by the mixture of diffidence and "hauteur" that characterised her behaviour and that spoke to him from her unsteady eyes.

She was not beautiful but her body was shapely and lithe, and she was of a fair rather than dark complexion, tending even to the colourless, but her eyes might have been described by unsympathetic persons as fishy. Rheinhardt looked splendid in his captain's uniform, but Marianne could see (she thought) a sensitive soul beneath the military stiffness. Thoughts on both sides, however, were stifled by the wordless exchange that took place, albeit momentarily, in the meeting of their eyes. This of course was belied by the veneer of politeness and the commercial transaction that immediately ensued.

Bélignan was aswoon in hot sunlight, its narrow ancient streets still, except for a black-clothed widow with a shopping basket shuffling along and a man in blue overalls spitting. Above, between the roofs of tall terraces, strips of vivid blue sky contrasted with the cool dark shadow of the streets; but the roof-tiles burned invisibly, and, when the sun got through the network above, it blazed on to the cobble-stones and drove its brilliant shafts against peeling paint and shuttered windows. To Rheinhardt all this was a wonder—a source of both pleasure and pain. He felt the temptation to lethargy, to lie like a lizard, prone and motionless, until a disturbance should send him darting into a crevice or hole; but this feeling was proscribed by his Teutonic education in hardy manhood and tight will. His Mediterranean posting was not for recreational purposes. Nevertheless, there was provision for a daily dip in the sea. Reinhardt wandered out of the maze of dark streets in the direction of the blazing shoreline.

He had no right to remove his tunic or peaked cap of course, so he walked anomalously on the pebbly beach like a marionette, his trousers outlined against the grey pebbles, his upper half almost absorbed by the blue waves. Further and further he went, giving way to the sultry temptation of the day, his imagination filled with the charm of Marianne, dwelling, as it were, forever in those five minutes he had spent in her company. In his present somnambulist state he couldn't tell whether it was the sea and sky and sun that was the dream, or whether it was the interior of Marianne's grocery store, with her as the central reality, which was. Eventually, sufficiently secluded, he removed his clothes and took to the sea.

This was indeed a deeper dream than his solitary walk had been. This other element seemed to release him further still from his painful human condition. He swam slowly, almost unconsciously, parallel to the shoreline, glancing at the unstable shore which seemed to rise and fall no less than the sea, the shore which itself seemed to become drenched from time to time as sea-water washed over the swimmer's face.

When he returned to dry land, he found that his clothes had been removed in yet another sense.

The story was all over Bélignan—how the naked German officer had been seen dodging, like a hunted animal, between barriers that might shield him from sight. How he had run, hecticly, towards the cover of the nearby *garrigue*; how a party of schoolchildren had been terrified, and delighted, by his appeal for help; how, eventually, someone had brought him a dressing gown. Reinhardt did not show his face in Marianne's shop for many a long day.

But the joke was not, apparently, shared by the local Gendarmérie. They instituted a rigorous search for the clothes-thieves, which involved the expected degree of brutality. But, after all, those clothes might end up in the hands of the Résistance.

Whilst awaiting his court marshal (for loss of military equipment: his pistol and identity papers, as well as his uniform) remarkably they left Rheinhardt free to roam the district. And roam he did.

He roamed the *garrigue*. This was a wilderness—infertile earth, hills, scrubby vegetation of thorny, spiny, tough and rough-textured shrubs, dry, dry as a desert, with clumps of Mediterranean pine (pine of Aleppo, umbrella pine, *pin maritime*) reaching their scaly branches in all directions into the bright air, air in which lingered the hot scents of thyme, rosemary and marjoram, branches whose shiny foliage looked black against the intense blue sky. And it was hot, so that you breathed heat as well as felt it; and silent except for the hum of insects and whirr of invisible cicadas. Birds there were none. From the high ground you saw the flat sea, agleam in blueness, the empty horizon, and, everywhere but southward, the fertile coastal plain. Rheinhardt revelled in his isolation. His soul seemed to fill the vacancy. He felt his humanity, his human conscious-ness, more keenly than in any other environment, above all in any environment featuring his fellow man. All his burden of guilt he felt free of; all his human anxieties. He was no more responsible than the air itself or the sound of an insect. He was sentient but conscious-less.

Marianne was dismayed to learn of "her" officer's disgrace but longed for a further meeting with him. Once again, he entered the shop. Her heart stopped. He was as courteous as he had been the first time, but she saw that there was darkness below his eyes, indicating worry, perhaps the anxiety that he had been able to free himself from when alone in the *garrigue*. He knew his fate, as a consequence of his misdemeanour, was sealed. They exchanged a few casual-seeming words, some of which told her that he loved to wander in the *garrigue*. She wondered if it was a veiled invitation. Anyway, she took it as that and determined to accept.

But she could not go by day. Too many eyes would be upon her. By moonlight she would go. She named the trysting place—an ancient olive tree, with hollowed trunk, where as a child she had loved to hide. There (she said) she would meet him.

And so it was. One moonlit night they made love beside the short but massive trunk, smelling the fragrance, hearing the distant wash of the sea, gazing at the cold stars. They blessed the War for bringing them together, and cursed it for dividing them. For they were the pivot of the Universe. And yet, all-important as they believed themselves, they wanted nothing more than a modest home, regular employment for him and children born to them in due course. Military glory, national pride, meant nothing to them just now.

Despite the warmth of their embrace, as time wore on it grew chill and concealment dictated that, for now, they should part. Marianne would guide her steps towards Bélignan, and Rheinhardt, setting off twenty minutes later, would make for his billet which lay in another part of the little town.

Alone with his thoughts, Rheinhardt cursed the War. He cursed Germany and her foes too. He cursed the weapons manufactured to promote war. He cursed the hands that wielded them. He cursed the ground on which warriors stood; and he cursed most of all those who encouraged them to fight. He cursed God for sanctioning war, because what He permitted He, by implication, sanctioned. Then Rheinhardt cursed himself, for being born to suffer as a tool of invincible forces. He cursed his parents for engendering him. He cursed the very air. And he ended by cursing all the ambiguous Paradise that now lay around him. Only Marianne did he not curse.

He got to his feet. Twenty minutes had passed. He began to trudge wearily towards Bélignan. Tears were rolling down his cheeks. He whimpered. Then he cried out in his despair. And he ran. Blindly he ran, wailing like an animal, crashing through the undergrowth, tearing his clothes and rending his flesh.

Marianne had reached the edge of the *garrigue*, when she stopped short. Motorbikes were roaring out of the town. Men were running into the *garrigue*, some with straining, barking dogs. For a shot had rung out, like the end of all things. A sharp detonation from the heart of the *garrigue*.

She felt two strong hands shaking her out of a stupour which she had hoped was death. But it was Monsieur Grau, the local butcher, grinning broadly and staring into her startled eyes.

"Boche!" he whispered. Then, with a triumphant shout: "BOCHE!"

Nest of Mice

George raised his eyebrow and they left. The room behind them echoed with voices. On the tables and floor were heaps of student essays, several dirty teacups, some ashtrays, a lady's handbag, briefcases and the odd magazine.

"Where're we going then?" said Andrew, pausing in the corridor to collect himself and deposit a thin sheaf of papers in the locker, the sight of whose contents sent a flicker of surprise over his heavy handsome features. Finally he seemed to reconcile himself to the sight, as to so many other commonplace wonders which daily struck him, and hurried out of the building to join George.

"I dunno," said the other, looking down and then up the street, with narrowed, half-contemptuous, half-vulnerable eyes. "I thought . . . maybe The Rex." His glance settled with mild earnestness on his friend.

Andrew's blankness melted into enthusiasm as his lips moved in a broad smile and his own dark eyes began to dance. He shrugged his shoulders. "Anywhere but here!" came the reply, in a hoarse whisper of exasperation.

Over the veal and chips, accompanied by Continental salad, they told how their colleagues had that morning revealed themselves for the petty, malicious creatures that they were. Each new incident was a source of new indignation and new hilarity. Yet George and Andrew were trapped. All they could do was take this petty, private revenge.

Later, George entered the Commonroom hurriedly, cursed as he stumbled against a briefcase left protruding past the edge of an easy chair, and, with head held aloof and high, crossed the floor to deposit his register in a rack. He was soon murmuring abuse of Archie, who was responsible for the briefcase, into Andrew's sympathetic ear.

"Well," said Andrew eventually, with an effort, "now it's my turn!" And he rose, laboriously, gathering his stationery together, and, with a grim grin, departed.

George's fingers moulded the vibrato as he drew his bow across the strings, his eyes closed in concentration. Beads of perspiration stood upon his brow. At the end of the performance the audience clapped politely.

"Double-bases rumbled like empty bellies," said George, during the interval, to a lady flautist.

"Considering our lack of an adequate number of rehearsals," she replied, removing the large glass of orange juice from the vicinity of her lips, "I think we all did very well."

"Well enough for that crew!" said George, jerking his head over in the direction of members of the audience, who were themselves consuming various beverages and indulging themselves in light conversation.

"Oh, there's my mother!" said the girl. "Please excuse me."

George grimaced sourly as he reached for another glass of sherry.

At ten-thirty he met Andrew in a public house and there drank as many pints of Guinness as he could before closing-time, regaling his friend with satirical accounts, quite beautifully shaped, of the recent concert.

That night George dreamed.

The Monster strode into the room. It was tall, shallow-breasted but male, with iron grey hair. An impeccable skirt of fine worsted covered its loins. Smiling affably it took pen in hand and began to call names, in a quiet fastidious voice, to which replied a variety of differently toned whispers. Then it coughed and said:

"We were studying the *Prologue to the Canterbury Tales*. The Monk."

"No," interrupted one of the students. "*The Pardoner's Tale*."

"Ah yes, the Pardoner. In Wordsworth's time, people living in cities pined for the country."

She had got up, was leaning her lean figure over the desk, talking intently, occasional smilets playing about her narrow lips which pursed themselves, characteristically, at times, to emphasise a point by the pause in the flow of her rhetoric. The Monster coughed.

"But the Monk owes his origin to contemporary scandals about which Chaucer's audience would be fully informed."

The students scribbled busily, with just a yawn here and there.

"The scholars tell us that this particular one was—"

Someone hadn't quite caught the name. "What was it?" she whispered to the student at her side.

He shrugged his shoulders. He had missed it too.

She turned to the blackboard and wrote: "Lyrical Ballads. 1798. Hartley. The French Revolution. Coleridge. James Thomson."

"But the Prioress is an exquisitely composed portrait of a nun," his voice droned on in exquisite modulations. "She is the woman of the world who finds herself holding a religious office." He laughed good- humouredly, like one who has made a quip during an after-dinner speech. "I know lots of women in similar circumstances! Ho, ho, ho!"

There was silence in the class.

"You see," she went on, "some people just cannot *feel* the beauty of poetry. 'To cut across the reflex of a star'!" She gasped. "But," with a little giggle, "if you don't feel it, what can you do?"

The Monster rose. "I will be continuing on Thursday," it said. "Be sure you understand the relationship of Wordsworth to the Pardoner before that time. And do me an essay on the causes of the French Revolution. You know that—"

"You know that—" echoed the beautiful feminine voice, "Coleridge couldn't have *lived* without the Ancient Mariner."

e noi lasciamo lor così impacciati

"What was the name?" repeated the student.

"What name?" answered another.

"Why, the name of Chaucer's Mariner."

"The Monster. I distinctly heard. He said that Wordsworth's Chaucer was called the Mariner, or, in other words, the Monster. Geryon Allessio de Interminei. Get it down. Get it down."

George Lewis woke with a start. It was nine-thirty. He packed his things, washed, and got in his car.

The little brown furry thing trembled on a ledge in Mr Meece's larder, then sprang to the floor and scuttled to the side of the wall. He had just opened the door in the middle of the night, to look for a biscuit, and, in the half light cast by the hall lamp-fitting, his bleary eyes were startled by the sudden movement. He watched, fascinated, half afraid. But you couldn't leave a mouse free in the larder! He slowly advanced a pyjamaed leg, then stamped hard on the floor. The creature shifted about six inches. Then, without warning, it scuttled into deeper shadow three feet further on, and further into the inaccessibilities of the larder. Mr Meece was concerned. Quickly he turned away and sought for the broom handle somewhere in the obscurities of a tall cupboard, then returned, wondering if the mouse were still there. It was. A lump of dark shadow, furry shadow, against the wall. But he would not kill it. No! He advanced the broom to coax it back into the hall; then he would, in the same way, "coax" it outside. But the creature refused to budge. How idiotic! How stupid to risk its very being by staying put! But stay put it would.

The night was quiet and Mr Meece was strangely aware of the world outside: the sky, stars, wisps of grey cloud. He could see them through the hall window, if he cared to look.

And the cold earth, the plants, the creatures within the earth and upon it. Even the occasional sound of a car interested him, because of its unknown destination, and its cold, night-wet metal. But he was in his pyjamas and he shivered.

The mouse had moved on. Inexplicably. But he sought it in the dim light, and discovered it crouching half-under the vegetable rack. He made a tremendous clatter and shouted. The creature dashed wildly between his legs out on to the landing; then stopped, palpitating. He could now see its little body, distinct, soft, brown, palpitating. He could raise his stick and beat it dead, but he thought of the mess of blood and bones. He tip-toed to the outside door and turned the handle. The mouse remained still.

There was freedom. There was the big sky, the stars, the wind. There was the Universe to which the mite belonged. Yet it crouched, trembling, indoors. Mr Meece hated it. He hated its stupidity and its cowardice. He leapt towards it angrily, shouting, waving his stick, knocking, stamping. The creature stared, wild-eyed; it moved; then sped into the night.

Mr Meece teetered over the tea-tray, whilst Mrs Stiller directed the spout of the pot down into his cup.

"Oh, thank you!" he said.

She smiled and went on with her self-imposed duty of filling several other cups.

He was a hypocrite. Whilst he enjoyed George's conversation and contributed to the satirical theme, often joining him and Andrew for lunch, he couldn't despise his other colleagues to quite the same degree as they did. Of course, he shared the two young men's belief that the rest of the staff were irredeemable Philistines, and he deplored what he thought was the petty bourgeois vanity of some of them, yet when, as now, Mrs Stiller was being nice to him, he was charmed. And he did, after all, have a bad conscience about the wholesale dismissal of all their virtues as intolerable vices. But he had a taste for satire too; and when it was effectively employed, as it was by George, he couldn't help but appreciate it and enjoy it, even if it was at least partly unjust. Besides, he had a high admiration for George's intellect and other gifts, not to mention his courage in confronting his administrative superiors rudely, if they crossed him.

Dr Durben came into the room, with a letter in his hand. He smiled, cleared his throat, and said, addressing all those present:

"Er, may I have your attention a moment?"

The hubbub of voices subsided and he went on:

"Er, I have, er, just opened this, er, letter."

He waved it in the air.

"It is, er, from, er, from Mr Lewis."

He paused for several moments, then continued:

"It appears that he has left us."

There was a murmur of surprise in the room, of disapproval, even of anger here and there.

"Why?" came Mr Binney's reliably unabashed tones.

Dr Durben looked at him mildly. He shrugged his shoulders. He smiled.

"I don't, er, know. At least, it says here—" He looked down at the paper, knitting his brow. "It says here that we are, er, all of us, a, er, a 'bunch . . . of . . . er . . . hypocrites'. In what particular respect we are, er, that, he does not, er, does not say."

There was a hubbub of annoyance.

"Flaming cheek!"

"Of all the—"

"Scrounging beggar!"

"Wants a good kick up the—"

"Er," Dr Durben went on, "the problem he has left us with, whether or not his somewhat, er, wild-seeming accusations are, er, just or not, is how to continue with the course Mr Lewis was teaching. He is— was—a good teacher. That I, er, think you'll agree, though—" He turned towards Mr

Binney and looked at him very squarely and expressionlessly, in the eye: "though his, er, inclination to complete his registers in the proper fashion and, er, to hand them in at the proper time, was not, er, among his, er, strong points! Is that not so, Mr Binney?"

The long-suffering Mr Binney agreed, bitterly, that it was so.

Dr Durben continued:

"The insult to ourselves, ladies and gentleman, is of no importance. Perhaps, for all I know, it is, er, merited." And now Dr Durben's face became hard with sincerity. "It is the desertion by Mr Lewis of his students—" He paused and there was silence in the room. "—that I am concerned about, that I am, er, angry about." He paused again. "We shall have to—" The pitch of his voice had now dropped to something not much short of a whisper. "—get in a Supply!"

He looked round the room, smiled here and there, turned on his heel and went out.

The bonnet of George's car bored its way through the London traffic, on to the motorway, then north. He was free! His destination was the Lake District, that Shangri La that Wordsworth had hallowed and made a refuge ever after for those who chose to desert the populous cities and who wanted to commune instead with Nature. George had always loved the mountains and the lakes and the big cloud-filled skies, and had never had much time for his fellow man. But his fiddle was bumping away on the back seat.

Dr Durben's moustache waved once again.

"He's come back," he ventured. "Yes, he's in my study now. Armed with a-a medical certificate. Pressure of work, apparently, too great for him. I can understand that. Ha, ha, ha! But what do you think we should do?"

Binney shut his mouth like a clam. Then it opened, bitterly: "Tell him to go back where he came from. That's what I would say. Damned if we should give him another chance. I consider that skrimshanking."

"B-but he is a-a good lecturer." Dr Durben did not stammer. His delivery was the result of Churchillian elocution. "A-and he does have a-a medical certificate. I think, you know, I'll offer him the post back. After all, the fellow we have now isn't any great shakes. And he's only here on a sort of sufferance. Perhaps the money comes in handy for him, but I'm sure he has plenty to do with his research. No, Binney, I think Lewis must win the day. Don't you agree, eh?"

"No." The mouth of the Deputy Head of Department twitched and he straightened his shoulders, his eyes on the wall behind Dr Durben's head.

"Well," smiled his superior, "I suppose you'll just have to lump it."

"I suppose I will. But you will be sorry. You mark my words. That ba . . . that fellow has never fitted in since he's been here. Always late. Never completes his registers. Damned rude—"

"Well, Mr Binney," cut in the amiable doctor, "I'm afraid Mr Lewis is not the only, er, member of staff guilty of that failing."

Binney smiled. "N-no. Anyway, if you want my opinion, and you evidently do or you wouldn't have asked me, I say don't take him on at any price."

Dr Durben patted his colleague familiarly on the back. "I appreciate your point of view, Mr Binney, but, like our Prime Minister, I am determined to *govern*. No, Lewis comes back, after a pep-talk, and the examination results stay at a satisfactory level, eh?"

Binney sighed. There was no use arguing when the man was being stubborn. It happened from time to time, always to the detriment of the Department and of the College. Still, he was the boss.

"I'll be in Room 5, if you want me," he said, marching away with a pale, bespectacled face.

"Now, er, Mr Lewis, I see you would be ready t-to take up your lecturing again, at the end of the week. Are you sure you won't break down again? You know, breakdowns are serious things."

"No, it wasn't a breakdown. It was just a sort of temporary panic. I'll be all right."

"Er, you are sure you will not feel obliged to, er, make a similar sort of telephone call in, say, a week or two?"

Lewis chuckled in his dry but infectious way. "Oh no, you can rest assured about that. I mean, I won't be able to pay my landlady if I do that. Anyway, as you can see from the certificate, it was a perfectly genuine case."

Dr Durben glanced at the scrawled document. It crossed his mind that the signature might not after all be genuine. But he was anxious not to complicate matters further. Lewis could do the job, that's all.

He glanced at his watch. "Well, er, I think I had better go and see Mrs Sanderson. You will excuse me?" He extended his hand. "Monday then?"

"Yes," said Lewis rising, shaking the hand, and cursing in his heart.

"Fucking good week I had of it," said Lewis to Mr Meece and Andrew in the little Italian restuarant where you could buy veal, chips, and Continental salad. "Walks in the hills. Peace and quiet. Good food. Bloody good!"

He crunched a mouthful of salad. "Yes, you should try it sometime." He laughed. "Feel tons better after a holiday like that."

"Yes, but you—" Andrew exploded with merriment. "You can't just clear off."

"Why not? I did."

"Yes, but . . . but . . . ."

"But nothing. Bloody good thing it was. What does that fucking bastard care if I'm away for a week? He probably wouldn't even know, if bloody Jenkins didn't tell him. He—" Lewis laughed again. "—he said—" His voice was strangled between laughter and the attempt to mimic Dr Durben's polished enunciation. "—he said: 'You won't make another telephone call like that, Mr Lewis, will you?' I'll say I won't. Next time I won't take the trouble to 'phone at all! I'll just bugger off."

"Dessert, gentlemen?"

The three heads poured over the menu.

"Yes," said Lewis, with some degree of hauteur. "Peach melba."

The other two looked at each other.

"All round then," said Andrew.

"Peach melba all round. Three," said Mr Meece to the waiter. "Yes," turning to George, "but you can't do it more than once. I mean, take that kind of holiday."

"No," answered the hero, swallowing a mouthful of cold water. "Next time it's for keeps."

"Yes, but that's just it," said Meece. "You can't do it for keeps. You can't *keep* yourself."

"Oh, I don't know," Andrew interposed. "You can get some sort of job. Somewhere. I mean, you don't have to work in a hole like that."

George took out his cigarettes and offered them. "No, you certainly don't," he agreed. "But the money's good. And I can sometimes forget the staff altogether. The students aren't so bad."

"So you intend to stay here indefinitely?"

"Indefinitely, that's the word."

Mr Meece began to anticipate the sweet.

In the quiet of his room George opened the black case and took out his violin. It was very late. Another cold Autumn night. It seemed as though the rest of the house was sleeping. Ping! went a string as his forefinger plucked it. The wood squeaked as he raised the instrument to his chin, his hand sliding on the varnish and the black rest knocking against him. He adjusted the pegs, tuning the instrument; then drew his bow confidently across it. He was pleased at the rich echoing sound. The little box was alive. Its innards vibrated. It was laughing at him, with pleasure. He chuckled himself. Then he turned the page of his music and began to play. Soon he forgot himself in the music and found, as it were, something finer. Heart and soul he lavished on the performance, eyes closing when they could afford to, fingers dancing, the right arm poised in action. On he went, oblivious, for fifteen minutes, before he became aware of a harsh voice calling outside his door and a fist thumping upon it. But he ignored the interruption.

"You are waking the whole house!" the voice yelled. "You must stop playing. Stop!"

But George played only the louder, more passionately. The hammering ceased and footsteps went away down the corridor. George played. It was two o'clock. A noise of car doors slamming. Heavy footsteps on the stairs. And voices again. George played. They came to his door.

"Open up! The Police!"

George stopped. He put down his violin. He stepped to the door. Opened it.

"What is this? A bloody Police state?!" he bawled at the amazed Constable and his landlady.

"Er, do you mind stopping that noise, sir? There have been complaints from neighbours and from your landlady. I'm afraid I must ask you to stop playing, or you may find yourself being charged. Is that understood, sir?"

"Yes," said George. "Goodnight."

The footsteps and voices receded. The car doors slammed. An engine started. And there was peace.

George looked at his violin resting in the open case, and he swore. He cursed his landlady, he cursed the Police, he cursed the world in general. He felt like an intruder in the world. He felt as though his blood ran differently from anybody else's and his mind worked differently. And he felt his way was the best way. Escape was the only answer, and that had been proved impracticable. What could he do? One thing he could do. One thing he could do right now. Something, it was clear, had to be done. But why he should do this he did not know.

The night was still cold and it was dark. Thick clouds obscured the stars. He dragged up the sash window. Then he took a chair and placed it by the open window, and sat upon it, looking out. Of course, the street itself was aglow with streetlamps—yellow monstrosities—and the very sky seemed to have caught a hellish tint from the town. He sat there, thinking, for perhaps an hour. No, he would not go to bed. He would not perhaps return to work tomorrow. Everything, in fact, was in the balance. All that really mattered was the outside world and the window through which it could be seen.

George sighed. Eventually he got up, stiffly, from the chair. He walked across the room. He gazed at the violin lying inert in the open case, and he took it out. Snap! went the neck of it across his knee. Crunch! went the belly under his shoe. Twang! twang! went the strings as they snapped. And he gathered the bits in his hands and piled them in the case.

By this time he could hear the house stirring again. He ignored it.

Heavily he strode towards the window and leaned out. He stretched his arm over the dizzy height, with the violin case suspended from it. And then he let his fingers slacken their grip, and the case fell through the air to shatter on the empty pavement below.

Hammering at the door.

"Mrs Thomas?"

"Mr Lewis, you will have to leave tomorrow morning. I am going to call the Police."

"No need, Mrs Thomas. I'll be quiet in future. I have just been destroying my violin."

She gasped in impatience and astonishment on the other side of the door. "No matter. You must go."

George heard her hurry down the corridor, muttering to herself. He went to his bed, and, still dressed, flung himself upon it.

The Sick Man

So he came to the bedside. He lay there, the
other, gaunt, emaciated, deathly pale, and
there were little tubes leading from his feeble
body into strange, indifferent glass cylinders
that gurgled from time to time. The sick man
was utterly their prisoner.

He tried to smile. But the dim eyes were so
weak that it seemed he were smiling into
vacancy, scarcely, timidly. Perhaps it was not
a smile, for, since his head would not move,
one saw the lips in an unfamiliar per-
spective.

"How are you, then?" said the Visitor
softly, ever so softly, so that in no way could
the other take offence, for they were not on
easy terms.

The pale lips moved slightly and he
whispered:

"All right."

There were other patients in the ward: a
line of beds stretching grotesquely far into
the distance, attended, for the most part, by
other visitors, and ignored, for the time
being, by the phantomlike efficiency of
nurses. Some of the patients were quite well
already, sitting up in bed and munching
oranges, like children having a treat.

The Visitor spoke again.

"I thought I'd just look in. We heard you were not too well. I hope the worst is over."

Was the patient watching him or wasn't he? Did he recognise him or not? Was he distressed at having to converse on equal terms?

"I think the worst's over now," he finally answered, through parched lips.

What could one say? The noise of a television set at the far end of the ward provided a theme for further remarks.

"Doesn't the noise bother you? Of the T.V. set, I mean?"

"Oh no. It's for the fitter patients. You move up the ward as you get better."

It was really too much. The sick man sighed involuntarily and shut his eyes. How fragile his hands were, lying limp upon the counterpane! Their bones showed all their brittleness, the skin shone almost like silk. Awful! The Visitor shifted uneasily. Better not sit down. Prolonging the visit could do no good. Yet would it not be offensive to go away?

"Perhaps you'd like some rest, then? I'll look in again, you know. In a day or so. Try to gather your forces . . ." slipping into a sententious manner he thought the other would appreciate, that he felt it incumbent upon himself to adopt. "Be a new man, eh?"

The invalid made a sign of acknowledgement, a faint change of expression on his colourless face.

Once outside, the Visitor breathed gratefully the fresh air, relieved to be free from the sterilised atmosphere of the hospital. There was green in the grass which acknowledged no kinship with the green paint on the walls inside. White markings in the road rejected all suggestion of a correspondence with the colour of medical uniforms. Birdsong admitted no possibility of sickness in the sky. The world outside was healthy, and the Visitor almost feverishly identified himself with it.

In four months' time the patient was released. It had been a perilous struggle with Death, and Life had won. The disease was much worse than had been originally diagnosed. The stomach was violently ravaged. Nor was there a reserve of strength to cope with the terrible wounds of surgery; the sick man had never been hale at the best of times. Besides, he was introverted, a brooder who dissected his own soul for the pleasure of discovering how sick it was.

Finally he returned to work, to the school which had, but in a qualified way, missed him; yet his spirit had haunted the corridors throughout his absence, for his influence on some of the boys was great. Everyone had expressed the proper sentiments, just as if the popular Sports Master had been ill, but it was all a sham.

So there he was—tall but twice as bent, doubly frail, as anaemic again. His voice wavered eerily, his eyes uncannily stared. Yet, his colourless bony face grinning with irony, his spectacles catching the light, he threw himself once again into the school's musical activities.

Then, one night, the sick man had a dream. He had gone, as duty master, on the usual round of inspection, which entailed his surveying the roof (which was reached by way of a dark flight of stairs at the top of which was a trap-door), for the boys made of it a refuge for cigarette smoking. It was a damp misty night and, as he carefully opened the little door, he was aware of someone in the mist, leaning against the parapet, smoking. But it was not a boy; it was the Visitor. And as the sick man made his way out on to the roof he heard these words, though he was not sure who uttered them—himself, the Visitor, or another:

> At the first turning of the second stair
> I turned and saw below
> The same shape twisted on the banister
> Under the vapour in the fetid air
> Struggling with the devil of the stairs
>   who wears
> The deceitful face of hope and of despair

The next thing he knew was that he was grappling with the Visitor by the parapet;

and then he fell, over the edge, into space. But the falling sensation pleased him, dissolving his dream into oblivion.

Next day, in the commonroom, the sick man, smiling, approached the Visitor.

"I dreamt about you last night," he said.

"Oh yes," said the Visitor, "and what did you dream?"

The sick man told him, and grinned, showing the even row of rather large, not very white teeth.

"Anyway," said the Visitor, "what do you reckon your dream means?"

"Oh, I don't know," replied the sick man. "I shall have to consult my analyst," he said, giving the last word an American twist.

The Visitor laughed.

But both of them knew that the dream represented the conflict that both divided and united them, each half-in-love with the other's ideal— "the deceitful face of hope and of despair". And as though to consummate that love, each of them fed his mind on literature they agreed best represented the spiritual alternative to his natural bent. So, the Visitor immersed himself in the writings of Kafka, whilst the sick man read D. H. Lawrence avidly.

Came the day of the sick man's retirement from the rigours of full-time schoolteaching, for he had secured a part-time position as music-specialist in another school while enjoying some prospect of freelance work as a music critic.

"You know," said the sick man, smiling as he shook hands for the last time with the Visitor, his colleague, "I will haunt you for the rest of your life!"

"I know," replied the other, smiling too, "and I shall haunt you!"

The Scientists

She was a dark-haired, foreign lady, small, with a rounded figure, and he was a lean young Englishman not out of his teens, very shy, but with a knowing smile. They both worked as Lab Assistants in a boys' boarding school.

She was married and had a little girl whom she sometimes brought to work, and with whom Johnny loved to play on the lawn just outside the long, corrugated shack where the boys did Physics. It was funny to see his stooping figure shake with merriment before the romping child, whilst Mrs Terence watched slyly from behind the bunsens.

He was a sort of willow-wand bending before the breeze of life, whilst she was the stout elm. He was just drifting through life as a twig in water, quietly, gently, making no impression anywhere, even enjoying the lazy existence bestowed on him. He walked with a shuffling gait, despite long legs, getting along fast without apparent effort, his head bent eagerly forward, though with an expression of dreaminess in his eyes. To some people he was just a sap; to Mrs Terence a subject to play upon, kindly.

They had long conversations at mealtimes: sandwiches and tea in the empty, evil-

smelling lab. Sometimes the little girl was
there, Susan, whose silvery voice echoed
through the long shell of a room. It was
quite a job to keep her away from the acids
and gas-jets, but she gradually learned.

Mrs Terence would rest her heavy, foreign
eyes, with the dark bags beneath them, on
the frail youth, and talk of politics,
philosophy or art. He was agog at first but
gradually learned how to make interesting
remarks, put his own point of view, which
was original and inexperienced, all in a gay
spirit of devil-may-care. He didn't take Mrs
Terence's talk seriously but it was
interesting to him like the buttercups
outside. She, in her turn, regarded him with
more and more curiosity, provoked by his
levity, though thrilled by the little flashes of
insight that shot through his soft speech.
Johnny Parkin had never been so happy
before in his life.

He liked walking to work on a soft Spring
day, on the stony path, between the old trees
drooping their feathery branches, with birds
warbling from them. But she came in a motor
car driven by her English husband. Johnny
Parkin smiled to himself as he walked, the
world was so ludicrous. What matter if it
mocked at him for his lankiness, his sallow
skin, his long hair well combed, his squeaking
shoes? He had it all inside him, in his lean

head, the whole world, whistling and twittering, brightly, like Spring! What did Mrs Terence matter? She was only one of the twitterings. It was like sleep. The schoolboys drifted past, in their blue blazers: like dreams they were. The staff houses sat like dolls' houses on the firm earth, wisps of smoke curling away into heaven, as though sketched. The rhododendron bushes gleamed in the shadows, great red splashes of colour from the heart of greenness. And the gold sun sparkled from a gauzy sky. However ugly the laboratories were, they could not counteract the loveliness that was everywhere.

But Mrs Terence believed that loveliness was a deception, unlike the laboratories that were real. Ugliness, she thought, was a testimony of substantial existence. It amazed Johnny Parkin to hear her talking like this. It was so unscientific anyhow. But he continued to play with her ideas as he played with the child, the buttercups, or his own thoughts. He was, quite radically, a child at heart. And she, with her dark eyes and softly rounded body, played with his innocence.

Eventually she seduced him, who had been a virgin before, and the experience both shocked and delighted him. What he could not understand was how it was possible now to behave as they had done before, how it was possible to go about their daily business with the images of carnal relations before their eyes—her naked buttocks, his scrotum and penis. How was it possible to discuss scientific apparatus or talk to the masters, not to mention the boys? Yet men and women were doing this all the time, like the perpetration of some gigantic hypocrisy, which other people called being grown up! Those very clothes we wore were a deception, a living lie.

Nevertheless he went to work and did what he was required to do, though he was somewhat awkward with Mrs Terence, who laughed at him for it. Once tasted, however, the taste of the fruit lingered in his mouth. He wanted her again—and again. She was not always compliant and they had their tiffs as a consequence, but they made it up, and came together again.

The venue of their lovemaking was often the laboratory itself, in hours set aside for the preparation of apparatus to be used for scientific experiments which would take place during lesson-time under the supervision of teaching staff, or they would arrange to meet there at weekends or during school holidays on the pretext of doing extra work.

There were three laboratories in the same building, with a smell of formalin, ammonia, or hydrochloric acid, all joined by an inner workroom which was the beating heart of the establishment. There the masters, Mrs Terence, and Johnny Parkin would confabulate, whilst the classes waited in anxious expectation. A bunsen burner would be flickering from one corner of the bench and a packet of sandwiches might be balanced on another. Bits of apparatus, like innards, were dragged from cupboards and led away into one of the clamorous classrooms, until, when the intruders had gone, the Lab Assistants exchanged a meaning smile. Such was life at the school.

And when the last bell rang and the herd of schoolboys clattered out, the building became wondrous again. Stuffed chaffinches and bullfinches stared from their glass cases, accompanied by owls and the tiny wren; fox and badger skins hung on the walls, like tattered tapestry; and a live snake slithered across its sanded tray. The Whimshurst Machine took pride of place in the Physics Lab, poised next to a model of an atom of potassium. The laboratory block thus became a haven of tranquility, a love nest. The lovers inhaled the polluted air as though it were incense and lowered the blinds against the sun.

Gradually they fell in love with Science itself—the mechanism of the Universe, the atomic structure of all material things, the electronic basis of matter; and they studied behaviouristic theory with regard to animals and its application to human psychology. They took delight in seeing themselves, and all life, as determined by grand impersonal laws. The idea of Free Will seemed sentimental and cowardly to them. They had no time for religion (which was superstition to them) or charity for charity's sake. They argued that self-interest is the motive of all rational human action, even when that was not immediately obvious. And, though many scoffed at their doctrine, when they chose to expound it, they found that few people had convictions of a nobler kind. Honest people bowed to their higher wisdom, whilst others stuck doggedly to a more comfortable doctrine in which they did not in fact truly believe.

And so, gradually, the love which had been innocent became corrupt: it was tainted by the egotism which their intellectual life bred. They made a fetish of ugliness, revelling in film of the more ghoulish aspects of insect behaviour, accounts of the "cruelty" of starving carnivores, the cold vitality of reptilian life. These things were not objects of wonder to them, examples of the diversity of divine Creation, but stimulants to induce unholy desires. The laboratory buildings had become a temple of Nihilism.

Mrs Terence and her lover looked round at the paraphenalia of Science in ecstasy, treating the various laboratory exhibits as icons through which they might establish contact with a Higher Reality, and, as they did so, it seemed that further powers were being awakened within themselves, telepathic forces, which enabled them to communicate without the help of speech. A germ of madness was developing in the heat of their dark embraces.

Johnny began to flirt with the child who became very attached to him, perhaps because he treated her as an equal, afraid of her ill opinion as of an adult's, instinctively giving her his being in trust, though she was just a child. It was his own childishness responding to hers. Mrs Terence watched curiously, wondering what Freud would have had to say; but, when she mentioned that to Johnny, he just smiled in her face and went off merrily, pursued by the squealing child.

Susan, however, became affected by the vibrations set up by the lovers, growing secretive and unwilling to play. She shunned the sunlight, seeking for her pleasures in the dark. The fair hair grew paler as the days wore on and she lost weight. Her father became anxious, forbade her to accompany her mother to school. He imagined the strange gases at large in the laboratory were destroying her lungs. She left them, the Lab Assistants, like a ghost.

Then, gradually, they lost the inclination to make physical love, seeking only the comforts of a maternal-infant relationship with Johnny lying in Mrs Terence's arms, being soothed by her. And so their love would grow warmer and warmer without ever bursting into flame.

And the Universe, to them, was nothing but a play of electrical force. They were like initiates of a high religion, where material objects merely pointed to a reality within. Their prayers were in the form of formulae, equations, hypotheses, theorems. But they pottered about their business quietly, so as not to arouse suspicion, deities of the scientific world. For they had gone far beyond their ordinary selves: they had become perfect embodiments of abstract force, fields of influence, invisible potencies.

They affected those with whom they came in contact, strangely. You seemed to be drawn and repelled as though responding to magnets, wire coiled about a magnetic core. You felt giddy, as though entering an extra-terrestrial atmosphere: for the shell-like laboratories in the green park had become the fixed point about which circumambulated the entire Universe, stars and all.

Sunlight became abhorrent to them, symbolising the vulgar activities of the daytime world. So, when they had locked the door of their laboratory-temple they walked hand in hand out into the night, under the stars, along the silent woodland path, their eyes and the sentient stars in their vastness seeming to join, seeming to echo each other, shining equally.

They had become a wonder themselves.

The dark lake which had been excavated by a later Capability Brown, and which adorned the mansion housing the main body of classrooms, shone in the light of the cold stars, silent but for the rustle of foliage lining the treacherous banks, as the Scientists strolled hand in hand around it. But the circles they described were growing tighter and the water was beginning to pulse like a heartbeat. The lovers knew, without speaking of it, what they were about. Joyously they clung closer together, their hands sweating with fear and desire; and an image of the mansion itself, the school, they saw reflected from the dark surface. It was their palace beneath the waves.

"We shall live forever!" murmured Mrs Terence.

"Forever!" Johnny replied, before they walked into the lake, which met them with Death.

The Latin Master

He was a man with a bold face, an extrovert if ever there was one, who taught Latin and looked like a gladiator. His visage fair shone with happy determination, for he was determined in all he did. He walked with a rolling gait suggestive of careless strength, and his suit was too small, to show he didn't care what people thought. He was out to uphold the Establishment, get rid of cant, and instruct his boys in the ways of manly decency. Cricket, he thought, was the best game in the world.

And he was always arguing, especially with the more aesthetically inclined masters or those who believed in Progress. For everything had been done in the past, he argued, by the Romans, or, if not, by the Greeks. And he was almost right.

He was seen to best advantage in immaculate whites staring down the wicket at a fast bowler. His bat would come fiercely forward, followed by an eye that glared menacingly at the ball, legs wide apart in a determined stride that pulled the trousers tight over his well-guarded manhood. He was very particular about his manhood. At the end of the day, sweat would pour soothingly over him, bearing witness to the worthy strenuousness of his endeavours. He should really have been a gladiator.

Yet he valued particularly his mind: its clarity and precision. Those eyes, beaming like a lighthouse, were windows through which the honest soul glared, for he never merely looked at anything. And the brows knit with concentration, the broken nose stuck aggressively forward.

The mind had its exercise just as the body had, in debating societies, philosophical associations, teachers' congresses, and Latin proses. So it was neat, elastic, tough like muscles. You couldn't beat it, though it was susceptible to some confusion. You might introduce unknown quantities that would puzzle it, even trouble it for a while; but it would always reconstitute itself.

And yet, for all that, the man was kind. He was courteous. He could, when necessary, smile like a courtier, however unpleasant the occasion, though you always knew it was a smile of strength, that came from strength, and went back to strength the instant it disappeared. It was like his love of flowers: he loved them because custom endorsed them for the purpose of gentlemanly compliment. You couldn't love flowers because they were lovely as flowers—that would have been effeminate (the gravest sin of all)—but because the greatest civilisation of all time,

the Roman civilisation, had produced poets
who had celebrated the beauty of flowers, it
was permissible for a modern Englishman to
praise them too.

Anderson was the undoing of him.
Anderson the weed. Anderson couldn't play
games, couldn't do Latin, couldn't fight,
couldn't even argue. He would just stand
there, blubbering. Yet Anderson he had to
teach.

Anderson was slight in build, with large
soft eyes and a girlishly smooth skin. He talked
mincingly (yet not without intelligence) to
his schoolfellows. He wouldn't talk to
masters. He giggled foolishly when he missed
a ball.

The Latin Master was furious. He took
him by the hair; he shook him; he cursed him;
he gave him impositions; but Anderson was
like the proverbial cork. Up he came,
bobbing foolishly; and the Latin Master
nearly burst with irritation.

But, worst of all, Anderson began to form
a clique. Unaccountably he became very
popular. The other boys followed him
everywhere. God knows why but they
followed him as though he were the Pied
Piper. He ended by forming a school club—
he Anderson! It was called the Classical
Society and it met, according to its
constitution, to study the vast contribution

Greece and Rome had made to European civilisation. Not surprisingly the Latin Master was suspicious. But as his suspicions remained unallayed, and as the work in his own subject showed no sign of improvement despite this extra-curricular support, he made Anderson stay behind one day, after a lesson.

And he bullied him. What was the meaning of this new Society? What did the members really get up to? Soon Anderson was in tears. And then he coughed it up. The members of the Classical Society gathered flowers, put them in vases, and prayed—to the ancient Roman gods!

The Latin Master nearly had apoplexy but he managed to stagger to the Headmaster's study, with Anderson in tow. There he disclosed the real activities of the Classical Society.

Now, the Headmaster was a big man with blue eyes, who had at one time been on the teaching staff of Eton College, which fact impressed itself forcibly on the Latin Master's susceptible mind but it did not prevent him criticising the man if his incorruptible conscience caused him to think he deserved it.

The Headmaster sprawled in his polished chair which was nevertheless shabby with years of use and fiddled with a pen. He was known to have a casual, mock-serious way of talking to the boys but he was subject to unpredictable rages, generally assumed (though the boys didn't know it). Confronted by this latest crisis he knit his brows and then gave expression to a devastating display of rage, which had the Latin Master as well as Anderson quaking in his shoes.

"Well, Anderson," he said finally, "what have you got to say for yourself?"

Anderson of course was in tears.

"Stop blubbering, boy! And speak up for yourself like a man!"

Anderson pulled himself together. He looked from the Headmaster to the Latin Master and then back again.

"Hic, haec, hunc," he said. "Amo, amas, amat! Amemus, ametis, amant!"

The Latin Master's mouth dropped open, the Headmaster stared.

"What," said the latter, in a dramatic whisper, "do you think you are doing— boy!" he suddenly roared.

"Speaking Latin, sir," replied Anderson timidly.

"Why?" roared the Headmaster.

"To show, sir, that we don't only collect flowers and pray to the gods, sir!"

"Are you in your right mind, boy?" roared the Headmaster again.

"I don't know, sir," said Anderson.

There was silence for a few moments. The Headmaster studied his pen.

"Mr Gordon," he said at last, "take this acolyte of yours out of my sight. Try to explain to him that this is a Christian establishment and that fragments of Latin grammar are no evidence of conscientious study. Tell him that, though his behaviour has recently proved to be delinquent, the boy strikes me as being far from unintelligent. Tell him," went on the Headmaster in this proxy manner, "that I expect you to be able to report to me, in the near future, that his Classical studies have appreciably improved. And now," he said, beginning to toy with his pen once more, "I am afraid I must ask you both to leave me for I must give my attention to lesser things, like the appointment of a new kitchen manager."

"Sir," chirped Anderson, as he walked down the corridor at his master's side, "does that mean the Classical Society can no longer meet?"

"Not to worship the Roman gods," his master replied with some satisfaction.

"But, sir," said Anderson, "what shall we do with the flowers?"

The Driver

He was a strong slim man, of medium height, with blue eyes and somewhat dishevelled blond hair thinning in sympathy with the lines on his pasty-coloured face. He was forty-two and dying of cancer, but he moved with the agility of a youth.

Claughton worked for a Jew in the textile trade, as driver and general factotum. He was a heavy drinker and a chain-smoker, and, before coming to Moss's, had never held a job for more than two years at a stretch, nor ever wanted to. But he was moody. He sneered at the other workers because they were lazy, and he thought Moss a fool for employing them and thus wasting his money. Claughton had a great respect for money. But he rarely spoke and never smiled, and so, though he was indispensable, he did not make for good "labour relations".

He was old-fashioned. He would not, for instance, drink a cup of tea in Mr Moss's democratic kitchen, but took it outside to sip, at intervals, while he painted the garage. Yet he talked "straight" to the boss, calling him by his first name and speaking his mind. Once, when one of his fellow-workers burst a varicose vein, Claughton was at hand to apply a tourniquet and stanch the blood-flow immediately, thus probably saving the other man's life; yet he hated this particular man because he was fat and lazy. Claughton was impervious to the sickening squalor of a floor and clothing soaked with blood.

But he was dying of cancer. You could see it in his pasty lined face, and hear it in his painful breathing as he heaved the bales. But it was impossible to persuade him to let anyone help him. He just refused, stubborn as a mule, and swore. Nor would he retire, even if he could have afforded to, even if the boss could have managed without him. The man needed work, and this particular kind of work, as much as he needed air to breathe.

On the borders of Lancashire and Yorkshire there is a little town in a dip of the surrounding hills. The wind blows keenly, in sharp blasts, from the heights on to the fields of dark-green grass, fields bounded by crumbling black stone walls; then blows into the little town itself, a town all pressing upon its centre, as though tipped inwards by the contours of the land.

Moss's lorry, reaching the brow of a hill, braked to let a car go by on the other side of the road, then turned right (first gear having been engaged) to roar forward down a narrow winding lane, with Council houses on one side and a stricken wall on the other,

finally to bear left into the cobbled drive of
J. S. Balmforth: Worsted and Woollen Manufacturers.
Evidently it was noticed by a man in a shed,
which stood just inside the open gate, for he
put down his newspaper and came out.

"*Moss's!*" shouted the driver through his
cabin-window at a pair of glittering
spectacles.

"Governor's inside!" these seemed to reply,
before the man who wore them took his bald
head back into the shed, possibly to "'phone
through".

The lorry moved forward to park near Mr
Moss's shiny black saloon which looked
somehow stranded in the empty yard,
littered with bits of wire, rusty bolts, two or
three empty cigarette-packets, and tall
weeds growing in all the available spaces.
Claughton switched off the engine, lit a fag,
and stared at the empty fields beyond the
wire-mesh fence. He was there a good five
minutes, in the silence, before he heard
voices. Glancing in the rear-view driving
mirror, he saw Moss and *Balmforth*'s foreman
approaching.

"'E can back it up 'ere and w'll tek it in
this way," was what he heard.

He didn't need any personal instructions,
so he started the engine, craned his head
through the window, and began to back the
five-ton green-painted lorry into the

appropriate bay. There a rope-crane dangled its two wicked and gleaming hooks over the space, suspended from a pulley in the vastness above.

"Does 'e want any 'elp?" a voice cried from up there.

But Claughton was already leaping upon the bales piled on the back of the lorry.

"Naw!" he answered. Then: "Tek it up a bit, will yer, while 'a loosen straps!"

The crane-hooks rose further into the air.

Then he had done, having slipped to the ground to unfasten the last of the securing-ropes. Soon he was back on the consignment, calling for the crane to be lowered, and fastening the hooks into the bales, then telling *Balmforth's* man to "lift up!".

On the first floor the bales were wheeled about on wooden trolleys and examined by the foreman.

"White botany," he said. "Coloured worsted."

Mr Moss appointed a "manager", his brother, because he wanted to give him a job, times being hard for him. But Claughton taunted him and wouldn't take orders, until one day he threw a handful of textile waste in the manager's face. Moss had to dismiss him.

But Claughton was indispensable whereas the manager was a dead weight; yet blood is thicker than water, and besides, Mr Moss's brother was a good gentle soul. So the boss was in a quandary. He asked his brother to try and "get on" with Claughton, but Claughton was undoubtedly "difficult" and the boss's brother without the wit to employ the arts of a diplomat. However, it was agreed that Moss try to get Claughton back.

He found him at his home, in a drunken stupor, but Moss was not daunted.

"I'm not too proud to come and ask you to come back to work for me, Bill—" he began.

"Sod off!" said Claughton in a thick voice.

Moss laughed, then looked serious.

"Now listen, Bill," he said, "you're too good a workman to waste your life like this—"

"I said sod off!" Claughton shouted, beginning to rise to his feet. "Yer can get yer bleedin' brother to drive t'lorry! I'm g'ner work for sum'un else. Not a fuckin' Jew!"

"Bill!" shouted his wife. "That's out of order, even if you 'ave bin sacked!"

"Oh yeah? Well, 'oo sez so? A've 'erd ducks fart before!"

"Bill," said Moss, "when you're sober, I hope you'll apologise to me. I can overlook this now because you're drunk, but I want you to apologise. I'm going now. Goodbye, Mary!" he said, turning to the wife, with a smile.

"Sod off!" shouted her husband.

Three days later Claughton turned up at the warehouse. He didn't apologise but simply started to sort "waste" with Moss's brother and the two women, who were working round the big basket. Mr Moss looked at him but said nothing. Later he said, addressing the driver:

"There's a job at *Balmforth's* next Friday."

"You can rely on me, Jim," said Claughton.

And indeed he could, for the rest of the driver's sadly short working life. As for Mr Moss's brother, well, he left the firm but continued to draw his salary.

The Kabbalist

The flames cast their moving light on the glass, behind which the Hebrew script snaked upward, curled, and formed itself into squares on the old parchment—words writ large and words in smaller format running in patterns round the central motif—set in a picture-frame, on the little table, with squat candles in tub-shaped holders standing before it, flames which made the letters seem to dance with a warm yellow life.

The face of the Kabbalist gleamed too: smooth, creamy-fleshed, smiling. His grey hair fell lightly and drily, in abundance, over his forehead, temples and neck. His shirt was collarless, of striped material, rather dirty; and his baggy trousers were pinched in at his fat waist. He moved gently, his voice was soft, and he smiled his wisdom.

He picked an apple from a bowl, looking at it closely, unhurriedly. Then he turned to the young man and said:

"Everywhere it is written."

His finger pointed to a mark in the skin, in the greyish-fawn colour that spread out irregularly from the stalk over the fine curve of the little green sphere, resting gently on a configuration—a pleasantly thick, warm finger.

"What do you see?" he said. "Chet?" He pronounced a letter of the Hebrew alphabet.

The young man assented.

"And what do you see here?"

"Shin!" said the young man.

The Kabbalist smiled gently, replacing the apple in the bowl among the bananas.

"You see, everywhere it is written!"

The family and the rest of their English guests round the dinner-table were taking little notice. He was an embarrassment; and his family resented the fact that he did no work, that he did not earn his living. His long-suffering wife—a wiry, brown-skinned little woman—let it be known how much she disapproved of him, for she was trying to accommodate herself to the new secular Israel, though she had been born and bred in the Yemen. He, on the other hand, had been born in Palestine of the Mandate, though his family had originated in Turkey. He was of a more European appearance than she was, who looked Arab. Mischievously his youngest, teenage, son offered him some more cherry brandy, which the Kabbalist, in an embarrassed way, accepted. It was his weakness and he was ashamed to acknowledge it. The boy took the bottle by the neck, as though it were a chicken whose neck he was about to wring, and poured a generous quantity of the liqueur into his father's glass. The Kabbalist began to drink it immediately, with a sheepish smile on his face when he put the glass down. His wife grimaced sourly. The lady guest grimaced in sympathy with her. The elder daughter of the house began to talk enthusiastically about her job as a shorthand-typist. The teenage son used bits of slangy English, of an American kind, to show that he was *au fait* with the modern world. His mother's elder sister looked askance at everyone, saying nothing, with her elbow on the table and her narrow head cupped in her hand, as though she had only now come from the desert, with her brown skin and dark eyes. Suddenly the husband of the English lady burst out laughing as he noticed the young man struggling to make himself understood, with the help of bits of English and his woefully inadequate Hebrew, in his conversation with the Kabbalist.

"He speaks English as well as you do!" he said, addressing the young man. "In the War he was in the Argyll and Sutherland Highlanders!"

The Kabbalist smiled. But he would not use the pagan tongue. Nor would he shake the hand of any woman, for religious reasons, much to the disgust and anger of his English lady guest. He was an embarrassment to his family. But who was the greater sinner: the feckless man or the wife who despised him?

The Fascist

It was a hot day in July when the little car drew up outside the filling station between Montpellier and Agde, with its black cathedral, a hot Mediterranean day, dry as a desert, with intense sunlight that made the white curbstones blaze incandescently and the dark-green pine foliage look black like glare upon the retina. Ants and lizards gave the only sign of life, crawling in the dust or flicking between the stones respectively, whilst, in the far distance, the seemingly motionless sea made a firm blue line. A patchwork of criss-cross vineyards and groves of grey-leaved olive trees filled the dry earth between there and the hard ribbon of road off which the garage stood.

"There's someone you should see!" said the burly, friendly pump-attendant. "A friend of mine. Just out of prison. But—" his eyes fixed on the motorist with an appeal for understanding, sympathy, as well as with a certain mischievous pride—"he was sentenced for political crimes!"

The motorist looked over towards the kiosk, where a sturdily built man, of short stature, was talking earnestly to the girl who worked there. He had driven up at a rather reckless speed, thought the motorist, who had observed him arrive, shortly before, in a cloud of dust.

"René! Viens voir l'Anglais!" shouted the pump-attendant.

Unhurriedly the subject of this call took his leave of the girl and strode self-confidently across to where the other men stood.

"René, je te présente mon bon client, Monsieur l'Anglais!"

The newcomer put out his hand, unsmilingly, and gripped tightly

"Je suis enchanté de faire votre connaissance, Monsieur," he said with a touch of irony. "Il est rare que j'aie l'occasion de discuter avec quelqu'un de votre nation. Vous vous intéressez à l'histoire, Monsieur?"

The motorist was feeling uneasy but he answered to the effect that, though he was of course interested in History, he felt he knew very little about it, having made the mistake of "dropping" that subject, at an early age, when being given that option at school.

His interlocutor was shocked. History, he averred, was the most important subject of all. Throughout history, he went on, delivering a veritable lecture to his new acquaintance, England and France had been at enmity with each other, yet, inexplicably (it seemed), they had been allies during the two world wars of the twentieth century.

Why was that? The Englishman hesitated, partly on account of his lack of fluency in the French language.

"Je vous ferai comprendre cette étrange 'entente', mon ami." He paused, fixing the other with a half-supercilious gaze. "Je suppose que vous avez entendu parler de cette fameuse Entente Cordiale?"

The Englishman said he had.

But, instead of making a disquisition on that, the Frenchman seemed to lose patience, as though too disgusted by the other's ignorance to want to waste his breath dispelling it. Instead he broached more recent matters.

"Pourquoi," he inquired with some menace in his tone, "n'aviez-vous même pas nous aidés à la guerre d'Indo-Chîne? A Dien Bien Fu? Il nous fallait une ombrelle aérienne, mais les Anglais n'avaient pas nous en fourni d'une? Pourquoi? Parce que les Anglais nous ont trahis! Comme d'habitude!"

His friend, the pump-attendant, spoke to him under his breath, so that the Englishman should not be able to understand, but it was evident that he was counselling discretion. Instead of being conciliatory, however, the other man replied:

"Non! Il faut qu'il sache ce que je pense. N'est-ce pas, mon ami?" he went on, addressing the Englishman who was gazing ostentatiously at his watch.

"Ah, oui, oui. Mais il faut que je parte maintenant."

The other looked at him ironically. "Mais non. Vous avez, assurément, encore cinque minutes?"

Though the Englishman looked doubtful, the Frenchman continued to speak.

"Dîtes-moi, s'il vous plaît, ce que vous pensez de la guerre d'Algérie."

The Englishman explained that, since that was a French colonial war and that the drift of modern history had been against the retention of colonies, it seemed to him that the French must lose. They had better make terms before the bloodshed became even greater than it then was.

"Putain! Vous avez tort! C'est de la connérie qu'on lit aux journaux."

He lowered his tone to something quite sinister.

"Savez-vous, Monsieur, à qui appartient la Presse française? Je vous le dirai de suite. Ce sont les juifs à qui appartient la Presse. Les juifs sont bien connus comme ennemis de la France. Ecoutez! Le premier ministre de l'état est juif! Michel Debré, petit fils du grand rabbin de Paris. Le Général de Gaulle lui-même est employé des Rothschilds. C'est pour ça qu'il pense à conclure la guerre avec infamie; mais, attention! nous allons le faire pendre d'un échafaud, malgré sa haute taille!"

The Englishman made a move towards his car.

"Un moment encore! Vous croyez à l'égalité des races humaines, Monsieur?"

"Oui, je crois à cette idée."

"Alors, pourquoi sont les juifs égaux aux français, mais les algériens ne le sont pas?"

"Que voulez-vous dire? Assurément, les algériens sont égaux aux français!"

"Alors, pourquoi nous faisons la guerre contre les uns mais nous ne la faisons pas contre les autres?"

This argument defeated the Englishman by virtue of what he considered its sheer absurdity. He got into his car and, with excuses for his departure, revved the engine. The Frenchman stood there, smiling, as if to say, "When we want to get you, we will know where to find you!"

And the Englishman drove away with the sour taste of Fascism in his mouth.

On the Bus to Sortino

"You see, I want to get married—"

Her eyes were wide open, a little too wide, and stared direct into the eyes of her interlocutor, with naïve sincerity.

"I want to settle down. Have a family."

She paused.

"Do you understand?"

"Oh yes," he said. "Of course. You are quite right."

"Do you think so?"

She continued to concentrate her gaze.

"Yes; certainly, I understand."

She smiled.

"You are so wise. How did you know?"

He paused, puzzled.

"Yes," she went on. "You know," she said, with a worried expression, "I am a very strong person."

She smiled.

"Yes. But—" Her expression changed again. "Very sensitive. Do you know what I mean?"

He nodded.

"Have you met someone like me before? Sensitive but strong?"

"Well . . . ." he prevaricated. But she did not listen to his tone.

She was petite, pretty, with nut-brown eyes, and short dark hair.

"Tell me," she said; "how do you meet the right person?"

"Well," he said, "it's a matter of fate."

"I never seem to meet the right person. My boyfriend— Pardon me, I shouldn't say this, but . . . we have sex just once a week now; but it isn't just sex that matters, is it? You have to be 'complete'. You have to be 'complete' in everything. My other boyfriend—"

She smiled, and her eyes rolled upwards towards Heaven.

"We were 'complete' in everything."

Her expression changed to the seriously sincere.

"I think it is very rare what we had together. It wasn't just sex—but in sex we were perfectly 'complete'—but everything! We liked the same things, we laughed. Do you like to laugh? I like to laugh. Oh, my first boyfriend and I, we laughed together about everything! It was so good. My other boyfriend, I mean. Do you understand me? I'm thirty-eight now. I want to get married. Settle down. Have a family. You know. But I never seem to meet the right boy. Well, my first boyfriend— The other one, I mean. His father did not like me. Because I haven't got a degree. So it is no good. You see, he couldn't hurt his father. His father is a sick man. Do you understand? So, tell me: how do you meet the right boy?"

"I don't know," he said. "It's fate."

She wasn't downcast.

"I love having a good time. What do you think? I'm thirty-eight. I should be more serious, shouldn't I? More mature? But no. Do you know, I love going about with younger people! In their twenties. We have parties. We dance. They love to dance with me. I don't know why. Do you think that's wrong?"

"No, not wrong."

"Do you really think so?"

"I can't see why it's wrong."

"But I just do. I love it! Oh, this is my stop, now. Will you give me your address? Would you mind if I wrote to you? Oh, thank you. I will write!"

Mr Doshi

Mr Doshi's wavy black hair was greying at the temples, where it grew thickly as it did upon his whole lustrous head. A glittering smile, illuminating his shapely Indian features in the round face, accompanied a husky voice that rattled too rapidly for his words to be distinctly understood, but he laid down the law confidently in an English staff common-room. Curtop encouraged him, moving his head a little to one side and then up, saying, "Kick 'em in the balls, Dosh! The bleeders should be taught a lesson." Then he would feel Mr Doshi's arm encircle his shoulders and smell his scented breath, and hear a whispered obscenity in friendly reply.

Mr Doshi thought the Establishment was prejudiced against him, because of his colour, and that was why, despite a string of degrees, he failed to gain promotion, but the truth was, he was contentious with other members of staff and incomprehensible to a large number of students. But he had the consolation of being Chairman of the College branch of NATHFE, the college lecturers' union, and in that capacity he lorded it over Dr Beddoes, his departmental head. Unfortunately, Union meetings, as handled by Mr Doshi, were inordinately long, so few but the most active members ever attended.

Privately, Dr Beddoes deplored Mr Doshi's behaviour, and he believed his left-wing opinions were harmful to the good management of the College, but he felt helpless to respond effectively. He would be accused of Fascism (despite the fact that he had been employed in military intelligence throughout the war against Hitler) and Racism (despite the fact that he had no objection to Mr Doshi's colour). So he took refuge in his habitual politeness, which Mr Doshi cursed as "a damned British impertinence, an insult to any intelligent man, the insidious weapon of the old imperialist Raj". And in fact Mr Doshi took his case to the Race Relations Board. Reports of it were in all the national newspapers and Mr Doshi was delighted. However, his case was dismissed as insubstantial—another proof (he thought) of the corruption of British justice.

Mr Doshi believed in the occult power of sex. He had read widely on this subject, in Indian and other literature, and he loved to amaze his audience with his knowledge of such esoteric, not to say indelicate, matters. He presented himself as a sage among simpletons, as a sophisticated Oriental among naïve Westerners. Particularly did he like to parade his knowledge before women; and he hoped, by so doing, to seduce them. Sometimes he succeeded. Often the objects of his disquisitions were repelled and fled from him.

Curtop's wife became his target.

There was a College disco and Mr Doshi was dancing with her. He was holding her close and gently rubbing her back with his flaccid hand, thinking to be inducing spasms of sexual gratification in her as he recounted several strange practices of an obscure Hindu sect. She listened with horror, though her revulsion from Mr Doshi personally was greater than from the tales he told. Despite his wish to bring this desirable white woman to a sexual climax by the sheer power of his words, accompanied by the rhythmical movement of his hand, the music stopped and both of them were obliged to leave the floor.

"Curtop," he said, on returning his acolyte's wife (he always addressed Curtop in this way, as though he were an Edwardian English gentleman of superior birth or greater seniority), "I return your good lady to you, as *virgo intacta*."

Neither Curtop nor his wife knew what the phrase meant, but Mrs Curtop, in defiance of all political, social, and ethnic sensitivities (and in full view of all present), smartly slapped his face; whilst Dr Beddoes, leaving the dance-floor with his arm round one of the fairest of the students, leaned towards the black face of his junior colleague and whispered: "Look to her, Moor, if thou hast eyes to see:/ She has deceived her father and may thee!" Unluckily for Mr Doshi, the whisper was discreet enough not to be heard by any but the intended party.

The Angel

I don't know whether he was an angel or just a man. I didn't like him, anyway. Who said you have to *like* angels? Abraham didn't, I think, get further than being ready to entertain them at his table, and, in any case, they brought good news, and they were anxious to get about their business. Something to do with Sodom and Gomorrah, I believe. Well, *my* angel, like them, seemed more like a businessman than anything airy-fairy. He came to see his mother, every night, in a retirement home; and he spoke in a loud voice, engaging as many of the other occupants of the home—so it seemed—as he could. He was quite burly in build, probably on the flabby side, with a bald head, glasses, and (as I say) a booming voice. He seemed like a show-off to me, so I didn't like him; but he was, every night, coming into the retirement home to speak to his mother. He spoke to her as though she were not in a retirement home, as though everything was, between them, the same as it had always been. But she was in a wheel chair: quite well turned out she seemed to be, and perhaps still coherent. Still, she hadn't got the upper hand any more and he had. He was pretending he hadn't.

During these ordinary conversations between them, someone might wheel a chair past with an apparently moribund figure in it: mouth wide open, eyes closed, body motionless, wheeled by a beautiful Philippino woman who would bend forward to wipe the mouth gently with a handkerchief, as you would a baby's. Somebody else's mother.

The place was full of cripples. Mostly, though, they were just too old for their legs to bear them without assistance from Zimmer frames or the like, and several inmates were assertive and at enmity with their fellows. You could imagine that, were they more lively, they could have careered about the building in their wheel chairs, brandishing long sticks to thrash their enemies with. But they were more sentient than you might imagine. There was an American lady who still made herself up like a film star and who smoked defiantly everywhere, though such was forbidden. Another, there with her husband who suffered from Parkinson's disease, spoke with a German accent and spent her time castigating the staff for their sloppy behaviour. But the Angel had members of a lesser angelic order to support him, though these were less conscientious—if that's what it was—in concealing their wings. They had dark skins, long black hair, ravishing features and behaved as though they had hearts of gold, though they might have been being merely "professional", for all I knew. They cared for the inmates; they cherished them; they behaved as though they loved them, leaning their cheeks upon the wizened old faces and smiling warmly. They were angels indeed—though angels paid and boarded and fed.

Mealtimes were a battleground. Doors open and the chariots would pour in, making for the long table where various salads were set out to be shared between the warriors; the next course would be served at the individual tables by two or three Russian ladies, at least one of whom maintained a sunny helpfulness through every emergency.

Meanwhile the sun shone strongly, brightly, from a pure blue sky, the sea was deep blue and the air mild. November in the Promised Land. But the weather turned one day, and there, out in the storm was a little cat, its eyes stuffed full of a grey discharge, tottering in the wind and rain, blind, unable to find food even when pushed under its nose. The Angel would perhaps have laughed, seeing a bond between the fate of the lost kitten and the storm of old age in the body and mind of people he knew. But he did nothing, himself fearing deadly disease perhaps. Rabies.

There was a synagogue in the home, to which of course the Angel dutifully went. He bowed with the little congregation, at appropriate times, enunciated the various amens, and gabbled silently the necessary prayers. Afterwards he discussed synagogue politics with members of the Committee . . . from whence he swept into the palatial reception area of the home, with its coppery square columns, tall, fitted with lights and clothed with mirrors, where sat the various inmates, chatting or in depressed silence, surveyed by the Russian receptionist from her desk, expressionless, with hair dyed henna. The town was drowned in languages: Hebrew, Russian, French, English, etc. The Angel woke everyone with his Manchester English.

I saw him one day in the shopping mall. The place had been bombed twice and I had sworn not to go near the place, but, when it came to it, I went in like other people did, and the poor folk who worked there for a living—beautiful young girls in the cosmetic and fashion boutiques, young men hauling crates of vegetables downstairs, middle aged women, men, the usual heterogeneous staff you find in a shopping mall, with, in this case, a supermarket built in. A slight young man peered into my bag as I entered. My Angel was examining an intricate necklace of translucent red stones from a counter with a wonderful selection of such things. Not surely for his mother! His mistress? His wife? Daughter? Who knows? But I was glad to see him there, because I thought the building would not be bombed a third time, with an angel in it.

How noisy the bedroom was at night, when there was a party in the rambling complex just over the road! Music blaring, voices calling, car motors roaring, children screaming with joy, dogs barking; and behind that the sea, quietly splashing its breakers on the shore, which showed up as a thick white line in the further darkness. And every now and then the deep rumble of a helicopter on patrol, watching for enemy incursions. The town was bright with lights and festive with late-night diners. The Angel was watching telly now, his mother asleep in her rented bed. She had an alarm gadget to call for help.

In this hall of death and the dying walked Stepka, fair hair coiffed in a serious but elegant style, lips brightly painted, never a change in her placidly enigmatic expression. She wheeled her invalid up and down, up and down. Unlike the expansive Philippinos, there was no love in her eyes. It seemed that she belonged in the pages of some Russian romance, perhaps of aristocratic society. She did not look Jewish; and they said that thousands of non-Jewish Russians fled with the exiles when the Soviet borders were opened, as ancient Egyptians fled with the Children of Israel across the bed of the Red Sea.

But the Angel fell in love with her. She would speak only Hebrew and Russian, her Hebrew being much more fluent than his; and he was filled with adolescent embarrassment. It was a moot point that his mother did not realise what was happening to her big son. He could not sleep; he avoided every eye-contact with Stepka; yet he sought her out. And she knew, of course. Nevertheless, her expression did not change, though she held her head, perhaps, a whit higher. She did not expect to make such a conquest, yet conquests must be exploited. She was poor, frustrated, and looking for an opportunity to better herself in this new land. Malcolm should be the means. He need not be the end. There were many youthful handsome men in Israel. She could see how shy he was. She must encourage him. Meanwhile, he was trying to summon his courage, so there was a good chance that their paths might cross, as it were, whilst she wheeled her invalid across the shining floor and he stood ministering to his in the other wheel chair. Their wheels collided, one day. "*Slicha*!" she exclaimed: "Sorry!" Then

poured out three or four other sentences the
gist of which Malcolm could understand as a
not excessively effusive apology. There was a
touch of reserve even in this. The two
invalids protested in lively discord, till all was
silent again and the offending chariot was
wheeled away. Malcolm had had time only to
smile foolishly and to mollify his mother, who
watched him closely. Stepka wondered
whether she had struck the match or
whether more friction was needed.

There were musical entertainments now
and then, in the home. The wheel chairs and
Zimmer frames and ordinary easy chairs
would be arranged as an auditorium, a space
in front of the reception desk being reserved
for the performers. Local talent would be
invited to spend an hour cheering the
inmates with popular music—light classical,
folksong, American "musical" songs, songs in
Hebrew, English, Russian. Perhaps the
Philippino carers loved it best. At any rate
they sang along, smiled and even happily
danced to the engaging rhythms. It was hard
to get the inmates to respond, though the
American lady, smoking, rose unsteadily from
her chair and bounced her left shoulder in
time with the beat, singing where she could
remember the words. Malcolm pretended to
enjoy it and jollied his mother. Stepka
contrived to avoid these shows.

As time passed a tenuous contact *was* established between the putative lovers, as Malcolm's clumsiness was treated as though it were polished courtesy and the faintest glimmer of extra animation appeared in Stepka's eye; but to all intents and purposes she remained icy. However, in her iciness lay her charm, so far as Malcolm was concerned, anyway. And, in a rush of uncontrollable enthusiasm, he presented her, one day, with the red necklace he had bought in the shopping mall. Truly she was shaken. She expected to have to work much harder than she had to claim her man. But she was overjoyed, which was told in a slow smile and very direct look, which accompanied her initial refusal to accept the present. Just as she saw he was on the point of regretting his haste, she changed her words to those of gentle gratitude. All Malcolm's loud jollity could not hide his confusion, his blushes.

So, after this, in some ways, unpromising beginning, they became lovers. But Malcolm did not find her flowering into a comprehensible and familiar bedfellow or companion. She maintained her unapproachable distance. She would not be domesticated. But he plied her with presents and tried to break down her reserve by pretending to treat her with a brotherly lack of consideration. It did not work. In fact she left

his premises on one occasion and only a long
process of wooing effected her return. He
would never take that sort of liberty again.
Stepka would remain her own mistress
before acknowledging herself his. But, of
course, she wanted him to marry her; so that
she would have at least material security in
this fickle world. But that step he was
reluctant to take. It would be like marrying a
tiger or, more aptly, a polar bear.

The women of the institution were on the
march. Some of them espoused the new
Feminist objection to traditional Judaic
separation of the two gender roles, which
seemed to belittle the dignity of women; so
they made a point of holding their discussion
group meetings in *their* division of the
synagogue, even whilst a religious service
was going on in the other (men's) division.
As a result prayers to the Almighty were said
against a background of loud opinions
expressed by healthy debaters beyond the
dividing curtain!

November gales came, sweeping through
the beautifully maintained gardens that
stretched all along the seafront, whistling
round the tall appartment blocks and hotels,
causing the proprietors of terraced cafés to
pile their heavy chairs and tables into tight
stacks. Umbrellas could not withstand the
onslaught, but the air remained relatively

mild. The sea was churned into frothing ridges of racing waves. The sky was grey. Birdlife and animal life had hidden itself away. The front doors of the retirement home, facing the western sea, were locked for fear they should blow in, and a side door was in use. Malcolm's mother was in the dining room. Upstairs, in her bedroom, was Malcolm with Stepka. They were on the old woman's bed. The Angel was undressed and Stepka in her underclothes was teasing him. He was laughing. They came together in the lovers' embrace when . . . . He was too old for these games, it seems. A terrible pain shot through his body. Stepka disengaged herself. Without thinking for herself—about compromising herself—she immediately phoned downstairs for emergency attention. Malcolm was carried away to the local hospital.

No one betrayed Stepka. The duty receptionist, a woman with hair dyed henna, was Russian too. But Malcolm was paralysed. He had to be wheeled about in a chair. He had become an inmate too. Stepka continued to work in the home . . . though, when her current invalid died, she elected to become Malcolm's carer. He thought himself a very lucky man.

A Wrong Word

Such a beautiful girl should never have married such an ordinary-looking man. She carried her head aloft, with a slight tilt, and looked down through the purpled eyelids, her soft fair hair touching ever so temptingly the delicate cheeks, and the fine teeth glistening ever so invitingly behind her full lips. Furthermore, she spoke with an ever so much more refined accent than he did, though it's true her family was in humble circumstances. Still, she had got on in the world—or rather with the world, like a house on fire.

Her husband could only wonder, wonder at her beauty and at his own incredible good luck in marrying such a girl.

He worked as a lecturer in a London college, and so felt himself superior to an ordinary schoolmaster; and, being a provincial by birth and up-bringing, he believed that his current location required of him a degree of sophistication without which (he imagined) his rather precocious students would despise him. So he wore fashionable clothes, poised himself elegantly on his desk-top, and discoursed eloquently on the subject of Saving and Investment.

The couple had lots of friends, believing that it was not wholesome to live just for themselves and that their marriage would be less subject to strain if they spread the burden of themselves among others; so that they might come together at last in a fast and warm embrace. Naturally, they were aware that to go out, thus, into the world, was to court temptation, but they considered themselves sufficiently strong to cope with that.

One day a colleague of Sean's rang up. Would they go to a party on Saturday night? They would.

"I told you not to talk to me when I'm in heavy traffic!" Sean's plaintive voice followed a gasp as he narrowly avoided a cyclist; but Sheila was too beautiful to be the target of his anger. She apologised so winningly that he almost went through a red traffic light.

Dilys welcomed them with cheese and wine.

"Now, I must just go and thaw out that spotty-faced Mathematician standing by himself over there," she cried above the racket. "By-ee!"

So they talked and they laughed until . . . .

"Why, that's Dave Mitchell, isn't it?" cried Sheila.

Yes, over on the settee, with a dark girl in a very low-cut dress and a fair one in a very high-necked one, was Sheila's old flame. A few moments later she was sitting in the place of the dark-haired girl, and Sean was lost in the crowd.

"Got any children," said Dave, "or are you on the pill?"

She took a long drag at her cigarette, half closing her beautiful, purpled eyelids: "How about you?" she said. "Do you use condoms or have you had a vascectomy?"

"All right," he said. "Touché! But you have a wicked tongue."

"No more than you," she replied. "Now let's talk sensibly, shall we?"

"Well, it *is* a party," he replied a little reproachfully.

Music poured from the loudspeakers.

"No, I don't want to talk. Dance?"

"Love to!" she replied.

Sean did not mind when he saw them bobbing among the other happy couples. Wine and music were exerting their natural influence (as Dr Johnson put it), and this was the spirit of the times. Yet, underneath his acquiescence, the young lecturer always had the feeling that something was wrong. He never objected or even thought about it, but, obscurely, when Sheila was dancing with someone else, he began to grow angry—angry and somewhat frightened. Did he not trust her?

"You're cute!" someone said.

It was a frail young woman, with wistful eyes and hair in a bewildering fringe. She had no shoes.

"Dance with me," she said. "I'm lonely."

So they danced.

Once, as he shuffled back, a soft mouth touched his neck. "His wife!" said Sheila's lovely voice to the impassive lady in his arms. "Don't care who you are," returned the latter, wafting her eyes to the contrary.

Sean laughed. "You're playing a dangerous game," he said.

For answer, his partner moved closer and laid her head on his shoulder.

Funny, he thought.

"Now I must go," said the minx. "My husband's a flirt."

Some forty minutes later, Sheila was sitting between Dave and the minx's husband, with Sean and the minx herself deep in conversation standing close by.

"The truth is," said Sheila, eyeing both men, "I'm having a baby."

"That's wonderful!" cried the minx, overhearing. "When? When is it to be?"

"In June," said Sheila. "Sean is responsible."

"Well, I should hope so!" laughed Dave.

"But you never can tell!" said the other man.

Frank Swinton drifted across. "What was that? What was it you were all laughing about? Come on. I want to know. It's my party."

"I was just saying—" the beautiful Sheila began.

But her husband butted in.

"No. That's enough. Don't say another word. I'm ashamed. You shouldn't make light of it. No. No matter how beautiful you are. Your beauty mightn't survive it, anyhow. So take care. That's enough. No more words. My wife—"

"—is having a baby," she added, imperturbably

There was deathly silence. Sheila smoked.

"Yes," she went on, "in June. It's Sean's fault."

Sean's head dropped on his breast. Frank nervously smiled his approval. The minx stared.

"More wine?" the other man enquired, in a loud voice. "I'll get some."

Sheila stood up.

"It's hot in here," she said, making for the door.

When she had gone, the other woman took Sean's hand. He knew she meant to console him. But she couldn't. Nobody could. Ever.

[Though fiction, the meeting described below was, chronologically and geographically, just possible.]

An Encounter in Riva

The lake glittered in the sunlight, and, beyond the band of direct rays, reflected green mountains. Lemon trees and olives threw their shadows on the terraces, where a sprinkling of peasants (one or two with his mule and cart) worked in the silence. Vessels rode at anchor in the harbour, or dipped gently as they headed across the water.

A summery crowd sat on the quayside, at café tables, where they smoked, laughed, and talked in a variety of European languages (though the locals spoke German and Italian): for this was Riva in 1912.

At one of the tables, a dark-haired man sat silent as his companion talked animatedly, whilst a woman at a table nearby eavesdropped on what was her native tongue. With a meaningful look and in heavily accented English, she told her own companion that Goethe was the topic of conversation—the fact that he, too, Goethe, had visited Riva.

"That makes two geniuses, then!" smiled the man.

"He's a writer, too!" the woman added excitedly. "The one who's talking."

Her companion looked. The man was short in stature, rather fat, with a certainly intelligent but not handsome face; but it was the other man who began to interest him. This one was tall, thin, sharp-featured. Not, in those respects, very different from the fair-haired Englishman who regarded him; but their facial expressions could not well have been more different. For, whilst the Englishman evinced keenness of interest in what lay around him, the German (if that's what he was) seemed preoccupied with what lay inside him.

"See," said the latter, apparently *à propos* of nothing, "how everything is reflected in the lake! Sun, sky, mountains, boats, buildings, ourselves." He laughed.

"Such is the beauty of Riva," returned his companion.

"Yes. But, as you know, I happen to believe that the reality of things is there—in the reflection. And what makes me laugh is the thought that it is silent, too. As though drowned. So, I must go down there, and look about."

"Which is what Psychoanalysis tells us we do in our dreams," said the other.

"Yes. But my dream rises upward, into consciousness. Always an anxiety dream." Then he laughed again. "But funny, isn't it?"

"Well, I don't myself always think so."

"Yes! Yes, it is always funny. Because the dreamer is beset by phantoms, whose absurdity he fully realises. But he cannot rouse himself from the nightmare."

"I don't think that is particularly funny," his friend replied.

"That is because you are sentimental, Max. For all your rationality. You should despise the dreamer. Not sympathise, and so, encourage him. Yet my greatest joy is to dream, with a pen in my hand."

"But you dream of God. And—"

"Of His absurd justice. He commands us to seek the truth, but puts obstacles in the way. He is as arbitrary and cruel as the pagan gods. Only they never asked a man to search his soul. In any case, I can't (as you know) believe in the existence of such a Being. But that doesn't matter. God is whatever rules us. The Police, the Church, the State, my father, even the whore I sleep with. Perhaps even myself."

By this time the Englishman was devouring the pair with his eyes, making what he could of their German, and listening to the woman's simultaneous translation.

"I like that dark fellow," he said eagerly.

The woman smiled broadly. She had wide-set blue eyes that sloped downward at the outer corners, as some Polish people have.

"I thought you were a creature of the sunlight," she said.

He looked pained.

"You are an innocent Englishman obsessed by an idea of darkness."

The man's pale face had grown paler.

"What do you know?" he burst out. "Your idea of darkness is nothing but a nasty effervescence concocted by Viennese psycho-analysts."

"And where would you be without it?" she returned. "What is all this talk about darkness if not a by-product of psycho-analytic theory? You may scoff at Freud, but you would have nothing to write about if you didn't know something about him. The little I've managed to explain to you!"

It was now the turn of the occupants of the other table to eavesdrop. The name "Freud" had caught their attention, as well as the raised voices and excited gestures. But their command of English was not good enough to enable them to follow the exchange closely. The woman's accent, however, had identified her as a German-speaker, which gave Max sufficient excuse (since he turned out to be as extrovert a personality as she was) to introduce himself, as soon as the temperature at her table had dropped sufficiently.

He explained, in German, that he, together with his friend Franz, had a deep interest in Freud's work, and asked whether her companion's criticism (which he could not help having overheard) was typical of "the English reaction".

"Not at all," she assured him, though it

was true (she said) that Freud's work was still very controversial. She smiled with some self-satisfaction when she explained that she had known personally one of the Master's most brilliant pupils—Otto Gross. At the mention of this name, the dark man told her that he counted Otto Gross as a particular friend. The two tables were then pushed together and a lively conversation ensued, in a mixture of the two languages. It turned out that there was a further connection between the strangers: the woman's sister happened to be the mistress of the German professor who had examined Franz's law thesis—none other than Alfred Weber, brother of the famous Max Weber.

"And what is your name, may I ask?" said the woman, more affable than ever.

"I am Franz Kafka," he replied. "And this is my friend, Max Brod, the writer. We are on holiday from Prague."

"And this is my husband, D.H.Lawrence. Also a writer. My name is Frieda, formerly von Richthoffen. And you," she said, addressing Franz, "must be a lawyer, as well as a writer?"

"I am an *employé* in the legal department of an insurance company," he replied.

"And a genius!" added Max Brod, explaining that Franz was, of course, a writer as well as a lawyer.

Kafka flushed. "I have published nothing!" he protested.

Lawrence registered the sharp features, the somewhat protruding ears, the wounded eyes, the fragility of Kafka's person, whilst Kafka was patently attempting to vanish before the candour of Lawrence's regard.

Noticing, Brod challenged Lawrence to describe his style of writing; but, before he could answer, Frieda announced that her husband was a "Romantic Freudian".

"What's that?" inquired Brod.

"That's rubbish!" snapped Lawrence. "I write from a totally different point of view from that of Freud. I arrived quite independently at my analysis of Paul Morel's sickness. And I wouldn't call it a complex. A complex is a neurotic condition locked in the unconscious, causing various life-crippling symptoms. The patient, by definition, is unaware of his condition. At any rate, of the cause of it. Paul Morel may have been smothered by his mother's love, but he wasn't blinded. And if he couldn't love Miriam, it wasn't because of his mother's opposition. Or, at least, that was only part of the reason. He couldn't love her, because she wasn't lovable in that way. Sexually."

"And I am?" Frieda provocatively interposed.

"Yes, you brazen hussy. You are."

To his exasperation, Frieda then explained that her husband had just completed the final revision of his third novel, *Sons and Lovers*.

"Paul Morel was lucky, then," said Kafka. "I am crippled. Yet my symptoms are few. A rather exaggerated nervousness, perhaps. A dietary problem. All provoked by the monster that dwells in me, consuming me constantly. I throw it delicacies now and then, to distract it. My friendships. My ungovernable libido. But it is no good. For the monster, of course, is myself. I consume myself. And without that food, I would die."

Lawrence looked at him, with intense interest.

"But don't you want to slay the monster?" he said.

Kafka's dark eyes met his, for the first time.

"How could I?" he said. "I am both the lake and the reflection in the lake."

Lawrence was putting those words, together with his impressions of the features and figure of the person who uttered them, into a putative drama whose hero would be metaphorically slain by his best friend—a rationalist entangled in a metaphysical web, unconsciously spun by the other.

"The condition Franz describes," Brod explained calmly, "is the condition of the race to which he, and I, belong. We are Jews—"

"I don't care about that," Lawrence sharply interposed. "Since you live in Prague and speak German, your claim to be Jewish is a fantasy. You are not dressed in sheepskins, worshipping the Golden Calf. You are sipping Cognac by Lake Garda, discussing literature and psychology—"

"I am a Zionist!" It was Brod's turn to interrupt. "Jews must have their political independence. Their own land."

"Yes!" exclaimed Frieda. "A modern Jewish state, where all the Jews of the world would go!"

"I hope," said Brod, smiling, "we shall have the right to live abroad, too. Like other people."

"Oh, of course!" said Frieda. "How boring it would be, if one could not meet Jews everywhere!"

Brod laughed.

"But what do you think, Herr Kafka?" inquired Frieda.

"I imagine," he said, "that if I were not a Jew, I would be happy. So, perhaps if I were to become a Jew as you are a German, with a country and a culture and a language behind me, I should be happy too."

"Herr Brod doesn't look unhappy," remarked Lawrence.

"Oh yes," said Brod, "underneath I am exactly like my friend Franz. Only I have a much thicker layer of skin upon me, which protects me even from your provocations. But come, we must be friends."

"I want to be neither a friend, nor an enemy," snapped Lawrence. "I want my independence, since we speak of that. But love is another matter. The love of David and Jonathan. That is the sort of friendship I think is worth having. Not the sentimental stab-you-in-the-back sort of friendship."

"Lawrence will not admit friendship with women, either," said Frieda, "though he has any number of women who think of him as a friend. And what's more, he writes to them, at length and regularly. He needs them. To hammer out his ideas on. Oh, he is selfish is Lawrence! Aren't you, Lawrence? Aren't you selfish? And don't you use me in that way, too?"

"You have me," he said bitterly. "The others don't have."

"Ah, so you would rather be free of me, too?"

"Yes!" he flashed. "I would!"

She got up from the table.

"Very well," she said. "You are free!"

And she walked away into the crowd.

Lawrence's acquaintances of the café table looked concerned, but he sat on, grim-faced, saying nothing. Eventually he murmured:

"She will come back. If she doesn't, there's no point in our being together."

And, sure enough, in a little while, the handsome woman, smiling radiantly, returned, with a little bunch of flowers in her hand.

"This," she said, looking sweetly at her husband, "is . . . for Herr Kafka."

At which point, she turned and gave the flowers to the bewildered man.

They all four laughed heartily.

Pensione Garibaldi

Pensione Garibaldi is on the island of Sicily in the beautiful resort of Taormina. Well, I say "beautiful", and so it is in a way, the way any beautiful place can stay beautiful when crammed full of tourists like me—the situation, high in the lap of a mountain overlooking the Mediterranean Sea, with Etna smoking in the background, and the centre full of antique buildings (many of them now boutiques), not to mention the ancient Romano-Greek theatre. It has been a holiday resort for ages, at least since the time of Goethe's sojourn there. And then we had the Lawrences (D. H. and Frieda) in the 1920s, the density on the ground, even at that time, of other *literati*, English and foreign, giving Lawrence qualms about finding enough peace and quiet to get on with his own work; but he in fact produced, there, a number of translations from the Italian, and wrote his famous Snake poem as well as the vivid long Preface to the Foreign Legion memoirs of Maurice Magnus. In fact, my enthusiasm for Lawrence's work was one of the reasons I chose to spend a two-week summer holiday there, just a few years ago.

Pensione Garibaldi was run by a Sicilian and his German wife. He was himself the

chef, and very proud of his handiwork
(justifiably), his wife operating front-of-
house, as it were, though he himself would
appear, in white apron and tall chef's hat, at
the end of each meal to see if everything
with the guests was satisfactory. He was
quite an imposing figure, even without the
uniform of his trade, tall and quietly
generous-looking. His wife was perhaps a
little intimidating, but together they ran an
excellent establishment. It was rather high
up the side of the mountain, making the
approach to the centre of the town suitably
dramatic—about ten minutes' walk down
one of the wide public stairways.

What made the dining room different from
the usual dining rooms, found in pensioni,
was the walls being covered with paintings,
amateur paintings it seemed to me. There
were some large-scale photographs, too, of
the family kind. But, on the whole, this décor
was cheerful, even interesting in its variety
of subject, yet reassuringly homely too. The
only picture that, to me, seemed out of place
was the portrait of evidently an Orthodox
Jewish man, dressed in a very sombre black
suit, wearing a hat of course, and set against
a rather lurid background of red paint,
unevenly applied. Now, I know "the War " is
a long way behind us now, and the Italians,
though pressurised by the Nazis, were not

notably antisemitic; but it was a strange portrait to find there, in a pensione part-German in proprietorship, and even on the island of Sicily, which had been in Spanish hands at the time of the Inquisition. Besides, most of the clientele was German. Traces of former Jewish settlement were to be found occasionally in street names.

However, I did not let this interfere with my enjoyment of the sights and amenities of the place. I would stroll along the Corso in the crowd, gaze in shop windows, eat ice cream, and clamber by different routes down to the distant seashore. Springtime had filled the green hillsides with flowers, the sun shone in a blue sky, the sea was fringed with sparkling wavelets, and in the distance Etna stood with its snowy summit against the sky.

Yet now and again something would disconcert me. I've mentioned the War before, but it's hard for someone like me to relegate it all to History. Not that I suffered in any exceptional way. I was a child in the relative safety of England. But now, as I strolled happily round the public park in Taormina, beautifully kept and dazzling with blooms of many kinds, I suddenly found myself confronted by a recent but to-be-permanent exhibit: a miniature submarine employed by the Axis, off Taormina, to destroy Allied shipping. A son of Taormina had served heroically on this vessel. Who can blame the town for wanting to honour him? And yet . . . .

Why I should find myself objecting to the music of Wagner, associated as it was with video film of Etna in eruption, on sale at a newsagent's on the Corso, I can hardly tell. But there it was, *The Ride of the Valkyre*, blaring out as accompaniment to rivers of molten lava pouring down the side of Etna, whilst fiery shapes and fountains of sparks showered from the crater. And another time, the mere glance at a picture postcard took me back to pictures I had seen of the inmates of Nazi concentration camps—for here were the decayed yet undecomposed bodies of eighteenth-century Sicilians, dressed in the rags left of the clothes they wore when embalmed, in the crypt of a Palermo church. A little further along the Corso was a pathetic postcard imploring the passerby to remember that such-and-such a man's son had perished in a German *lago*. But I had come here for D. H. Lawrence's sake too, so off I went to gaze at the outside of the villa he and Frieda had rented.

So, here it was, Fontana Vecchia, looking northward up the coast, high, high up above the sea, as was all Taormina, with a plaque upon the tall blank red-painted wall. Right on the edge of town. You couldn't go much further, even though new residential building sites occupied the level immediately above. I was like any other pilgrim visiting a "sacred" spot, full of inexplicable feelings, trying to reverse the flow of Time, just for a few minutes; and, like the others, I was glad to have been there and disappointed that Time insisted on flowing on. So, back to the Pensione Garibaldi for dinner.

I had noticed, during the few days I had already lodged at the Garibaldi, a somewhat elderly man, evidently a friend or perhaps relative of the proprietors, who sat in the lounge and often played a board game with the little girl who seemed to belong to the house, as one of the family. You know how it is. You get curious about certain people. Perhaps make up stories about them in your mind, imagining you can plumb their characters, understand them; and all kinds of exotic permutations can follow. Well, this man so caught my fancy. Who was he? It is difficult, in Southern countries, to guess whether someone is of Hebrew race, because the generally darker hair and eye colour, if not the browner skin, may give the impression of a Hebrew origin when in actuality it means nothing of the kind; and even the Semitic nose is no sure guide, anywhere, though it is certainly commoner among Jews than non-Jews. Besides, I never got the opportunity to observe this man face to face, which I mention because the expression of the eyes might tell something to someone who knows about these things. (But one should keep silent about these things, so close as we are to the century which brought forth the Holocaust.)

But I was uncomfortable. Every time I came back to the pensione for a meal I found myself staring at that tragic face—for the face in the painting was tragic. And at the same time I was surrounded by people speaking German. The room was awash with the German language, loud, boisterous, guttural, good-humoured so far as I knew. No melodic Italian, fastidious French, careful English, except perhaps the odd voice, like a voice drowning in a sea of German. To make matters worse (or better, I'm not sure which) I struck up a rather jolly dinner-time relationship with a young man from Bavaria. His English was deeply fractured and my German was non-existent, but we joked and felt a certain brotherly warmth. He was clearly having a very good time, with a pretty lady-friend to accompany him. He drank a lot and laughed a lot, yet if the whole room had been full of his replicas, I should have been more than overwhelmed. The trouble was, I didn't know the other guests: all I had was the sound of their voices.

My first Sunday in Taormina was Palm Sunday. There was a procession along the Corso: the priest in robes carrying the Cross, little boys in surplices, followed by other men, women and children in their best clothes, green palm leaves waving above along the narrow street, beneath a uniformly blue sky from which a hot sun poured down its golden light, hand-bells ringing. And the crowd of holiday makers and other people craned their necks to see, crowded into doorways.

Another day I took a coach-trip to the summit of Etna. It was like approaching Heaven in reverse. As you neared the top you found yourself in a desert of solidified lava, some of it still warm; grey ash; all the lush vegetation and cultivation left behind, the temperature falling as you rose higher into the thinner air; then snow, veritable white blinding snow. Heaven was below.

But I was not at my ease. I should have been celebrating the exodus of my people from Egypt, some 3,500 years before.

What I put into my mouth was itself an abomination, because it was not prepared according to special Passover specifications, let alone according to the ordinary laws of *kashrut*; but it was all my own fault. No one told me to take a holiday at this time of the year. However, I had brought with me my

traditional prayer-shawl in case there should
be a synagogue in Taormina. There was not.
But it would soon be Good Friday and then
Easter.

"Do you . . . ." It was after dinner on
Thursday. "Are you . . . . Do you happen to be
Jewish?" It was the old man who sometimes
played board games with the little girl.
Though he spoke to me in English his
accent was German. Then I saw that he too
was a Jew.

"Well yes, but why do you ask?"

"It is *pesach* now——" he used the Hebrew
word (perhaps to persuade me that he wasn't
an impostor). "And so I just wondered, well,
wondered if you were perhaps 'observant'
and had thought of attending a synagogue . . .
although there isn't one here," he quickly
added.

I was surprised at the soundness of his
intuition, yet he had one of those serious
intelligent faces that old men who have
thought much, and perhaps suffered much,
sometimes do have; so I was more humbled
than quizzical.

"Well yes, I did think of it," I said, "but
found none."

"No, no. Well . . . ." he looked down, with
the ghost of a smile on his lips. "This was
Spanish territory, you know. The Inquisition
did its work well."

"You mean there hasn't been a synagogue since 1492?"

He didn't answer but began to walk in the direction of the open door, inviting me to follow. Outside the night was beautiful. You could see the lights of the town below and the edge of the sea lapping against the shore. He directed my gaze away to the right and higher than the level we were standing on, in the direction of Etna. All seemed dark there.

"Look," he said, "still higher and a little more to the right. Do you see anything?"

I could see nothing but perhaps the dark flank of the mountain; at least I could see its outline against the sky if I chose to.

"Keep your eyes fixed on the darkness," he said. "You will see."

And then I did: the small flickering of a flame.

"Yes," he said, before I had spoken, but I suppose my body stiffened and gave him the clue. "Yes, you can see the fire."

"What does it mean?" I said, nervous. "Is it dangerous?"

"Who can tell? And then, dangerous for whom? Taormina is not much in range, but Catania is and the villages on the mountain sides. There is a small eruption. Who knows if it will grow. You have seen the images on the Corso, haven't you, film of the mountain in full blazing eruption? That's what people really want to happen, so long as they are personally out of range. It will give this island still more fascination for the tourist, and if there are many dead, well, think of all the solemn memorial services there will be in the churches. The Prime Minister will perhaps come down here from Rome. Perhaps the Pope himself. Everyone will have a very good dinner out of it."

"You are very cynical," I said.

"Cynical! Cynical! What do you mean cynical? Have you ever been in Hell?"

"I'm sorry," I stammered. "I must have touched a raw nerve."

He had calmed down.

"No, I'm sorry," he said. "I should have more self-control. But then—" he smiled, "I am not English!"

We sauntered once or twice along the terrace and back.

"You were asking me about synagogues," I remarked.

He waited a few seconds before replying.

"Synagogue, synagogue, yes. I believe you 'observant' Jews wear prayer-shawls in your synagogues."

I was disconcerted by the way he had suddenly distanced himself from me and in fact from his very race.

"Yes, well. Do you have one with you, yours?"

"I do. Why?"

"Well, will you lend it to me?"

Now it was my turn to pause. I didn't want to "lend" my prayer-shawl to anyone, least of all a stranger, and one I felt I didn't, into the bargain, understand. My prayer-shawl was, to my mind, more personal—if I may make so crude a comparison—more personal than my underpants. It was part of my soul, if I can put it that way, without wanting to make out that I am an especially pious person. Call it superstition if you like. Hesitantly I asked him what he wanted it for?

"To paint," he said. "I want to wrap myself in it and paint my own portrait like Rembrandt!"

He was joking about the Rembrandt bit but the general idea . . . .

"Yes, yes," he said, quite serious now. "You have seen many of my paintings on the walls of this Sicilian pensione, so efficiently run by my half-Jewish cousin Giorgio."

The bitterness of the latter part of his comment was, at the moment, inexplicable to me, though it hinted at an intriguing tale.

"And you have, I'm sure, noticed the portrait I painted of my late father, who perished in Auschwitz."

I hung my head. "Alav ha'shalom," I muttered (peace be upon him). "By all means borrow the *tallit*. Come to my room now and you can have it."

Carlo Ricardo returned to the modest villa he occupied, not far from the Pensione Garibaldi but even higher up the hill. The "new" developments lined the road that zig-zagged ever higher up the cone of the mountain, weaving sideways as far as was practicable then snaking back and up; and between the long curves were, at suitable intervals, dizzying stairways rising vertically to join the different levels. Carlo plodded up one of these, conscious that in his pocket was a little velvet bag containing the shawl, and this made his head spin slightly, as though he had drunk too much wine. For the shawl was, he felt, a sacred object, or at any rate was treated as such by those who, unlike himself, "believed"; and he could sense the centuries, nay millennia, of belief that permeated it, sensed it all the more because he stood outside the congregation that adhered to it, though, because he had been born within that congregation, he felt too (almost proudly) that he had a right to possess the broad, white silk scarf, with the parallel blue bands at the two ends, just above the long fringes, that constituted the prayer-shawl. But the purpose he intended for it caused his head to swim the more. If he looked behind himself and down, he would have plenty of physical cause for giddiness, but it was the fall in his head that caused the sensation.

He reached his dwelling and took off his jacket; then he wandered into the kitchen to make himself some coffee. He could hear music from a neighbouring property and the noise of traffic on the "boulevard"; but there was no voice to welcome him home, or even a dog or cat. But he was distracted from his loneliness by the activity of making the coffee and carrying it into his sitting room, which, like the pensione, was hung with pictures; however, photographs were confined to his mantelpiece and a small upright piano. They were all of a previous generation—his parents, his grandparents, his uncles and aunts, albeit with a sprinkling of his cousins as children in the family groups, himself included. He stopped, with the cafetière still in his hand, to look intently at the group consisting of his Aunt "Coco" (his pet-name for his Aunt Hannah) and her husband, a tall, dark-haired man, smiling broadly; and there was Giorgio too, their son and presently proprietor of the Pensione Garibaldi.

He turned away and sat down, after first switching on the television set; but he did not turn up the volume, so that faces were seen, filling the gaudy screen but mouthing meaninglessly at one another. Carlo sat sipping his coffee and looking with glazed eyes at the screen. His thoughts were elsewhere.

Having finished his coffee, he carried the pots into the kitchen, washed them up, dried them and put them away. He was meticulous in his habits. He then took a deep breath, smoothed his hands over each other for a few moments, as though washing or caressing them, went to the wardrobe in the lobby where he had left his jacket, carefully removed the velvet *tallit* bag, which was ornamented with an embroidered Shield of David, and went upstairs.

There he entered his studio, with its broad skylight and great window, with blinds to close against a too glaring light. There was no furniture but an easel, a chair, and some canvases, primed and unprimed, some with unfinished paintings on them, and a full-length mirror in a dusty gilt frame. The floor was uncarpeted, made of boards, and stained with paint. Here was an appearance of dis-order, but it was only the natural order of a mind devoted to one end—painting. Carlo took a deep breath. Yes, this place was like no other. What filled his lungs was the aroma of paint and turpentine, the ingredients of his trade, his art, his mystery. He stood for a minute or two in the relative emptiness, enjoying the buoyancy this echoing shell gave to his bones, his blood. The dizziness was gone. Instead, a quiet and steady determination took possession of him. He left the room and came back dressed in a dark suit, a trilby hat on his head. He opened the velvet bag and drew forth the mysterious garment, swung it over his shoulders, and looked at himself in the mirror. He removed the shawl and his jacket, donned a paint-splashed overall and began to mix his paints.

I learned later what the story was, the background to the ensuing events. Giorgio's father—Carlo's uncle—had met his "Auntie Coco" in Germany before the War. When the persecution began, Carlo's parents (like the rest of his family) were despatched to the camps. "Auntie Coco" was sent too, but Cesare (her husband by this time, and father of her four-year old little boy, Giorgio) was left at liberty to look after him, because he was an Italian citizen and "Aryan". Carlo, by special request of the Italian ambassador responding to the passionate pleas of Cesare, was permitted to move in with them. Though this saved the child's life and enabled him in due course to leave Germany with his uncle and cousin, Carlo never forgave his uncle for not saving his Aunt Coco, however impossible such a rescue might have been. He was a child, and as such could not comprehend the fate to which his family was subject, and resented bitterly the seeming invulnerability of his Aryan uncle. Carlo's mind had been unhinged by the world into which he had been born, and, above all, by the fate of his aunt, whom he loved more than any other human being. She had seemed the soul of gentleness to him. Her warmth and her smile gave Love its meaning for him.

Carlo went on painting through the night. He had dragged a couple of spotlights and a reading lamp into his studio and positioned them strategically, so as to throw light and shade where he wanted it. This portrait would be at least technically more subtle than the juvenile one of his father. But as he stared in the glass at his own face, his confidence began to drain away. Who was he? What was he hoping to achieve? With an effort he turned his attention to other parts of the composition, approaching the work with the objective concentration of a craftsman. And his patience was rewarded. The image on the canvas began to breathe with life; the colours began to glow. For this was no mere black-and-red job, the lurid colours of blood and death. Over the years Carlo had grown in experience of his craft,

which was at the same time a growth in the
clarity of his vision, a clarity that depended
on complexity, complexity of recognition
that it was from the mysterious mingling of
the colours of the whole spectrum that living
colour was made. Just as the glorious light of
the Sicilian sun split into fragments as it
touched the blue waves, so were the bristles
of his painter's brush able to scatter a myriad
tinctures on the canvas, the world which he
was creating, a creation further intensified by
the play of ordinary light and shade. But
sooner or later he would have, once again, to
look into his own eyes. What did he see
there? A darkness, an inchoate darkness. For
a moment he wondered whether or not he
might paint that: a world of light with a
darkness at the centre, a man whose soul was
dead. He shuddered. Nevertheless, he
continued to paint, to paint the darkness, for
he knew by now that darkness was not just
an absence of light, and even if it was, you
could not just leave a hole in the canvas. Not
he. No, he had to study the relationship
between the pigments he had already applied
to the face and discover where the boundary
of darkness actually was in relationship to
them; then begin to find a new combination
of shades to render it, ever deepening, ever
deepening, deepening into eternity, an
eternity of darkness, as far as Hell, even unto

Hell. So, with the electric light burning and the hours lengthening, with the moon rising and falling in the sky, the stars flashing, the waves eternally splashing on the shore hundreds of metres below, below the twinkle of lights from the town, Carlo went on working, trying to solve his technical problems and trying to face up to the truth about himself.

It was dawn. It was Good Friday. Carlo put down his brush, exhausted. He dragged his feet to his bedroom and threw himself, as he was, on the bed. Mercifully sleep came to him at once, and he remained where he was till early evening. Suddenly he looked at his watch and jumped to his feet. A quick wash, a shave, a change of clothes . . . . He had promised to play a game with Lucia, Giorgio's daughter, before dinner. He left the house and hurried carelessly down the long vertical stairway to the level on which stood the Pensione Garibaldi. She was waiting for him. "Uncle Carlo! Uncle Carlo, where have you been?" He kissed her and they settled down to play. Several guests were already on the premises. I happened to be one of them. He caught my eye and smiled. I returned his smile, thinking he looked a little brighter than usual, less sombre; but clearly the little girl liked him however he was. I strolled on the terrace, chatted to my Bavarian friend, gazed at the wonderful view below, which never lost its charm, then at the flank of Etna. Yes, it was still fiery in one place. Of course, the other guests knew about the eruption by now, and those who were present spoke about it excitedly. So far, no harm had come of it, though the village nearest to the fire and smoke was taking worried precautions, the local newspaper said. It also said that excursions were available for people to see the eruption at close quarters.

It is amazing how important meals become when one is on holiday. I was absurdly impatient to get at mine. I looked forward to a generous quantity of good red wine too. At last, I was seated at table, with a spotless white cloth before me and gleaming silver cutlery. All ready for the feast! I couldn't help but enjoy it when it came.

Then, afterwards, I lingered in the lounge, took a cup of coffee there, joined several people gazing at the television news programme, caught a fleeting glimpse on screen of Taormina and the wounded side of Etna (viewed from a light aircraft), yawned a few times, but thought I ought to make more use of the evening than just retire to bed; so I took a slow walk into town and joined the throng parading along the Corso. I returned to the pensione at about ten-fifteen and went to bed. In the middle of the night—actually it was three o'clock in the morning—I was awakened by screams and the sound of hurried footsteps. I put on my dressing gown and cautiously opened my bedroom door. A police officer was standing there about to knock. I had to dress and accompany him to the police station. There I was confronted with my prayer-shawl, torn and blood-stained. It had been used as a murder weapon. Carlo had murdered his uncle, who—though I had no need to have known it—lived at the Garibaldi.

Carlo had spent the rest of the evening, as usual, at the Garibaldi, eating there and sitting with the rest of the family, including his Uncle Cesare. He even told them that he was painting a new picture, a painting of himself. They took a polite interest but none of them thought he had any real talent. They were just wondering where they would have to put yet another dud painting. But Carlo was unusually excited; at least as unusually excited as he always was when he had started a new picture. As we know, they never came to anything. He was, everyone agreed, slightly unhinged. The War had done it. Who could wonder? Let alone who could blame him? His Uncle Cesare had tried to interest him in the hotel business, but it was no good.

Carlo had the most ridiculous ambitions, totally unrealistic. How could he earn a living by painting? Well, he might make something by doing tourist views of Taormina—and indeed he had tried his hand at that (some examples were on the walls of the Garibaldi)—but he had no persistence. He was a man who seemed incapable of accepting his own limitations. And that was because he wasn't content with the common lot of Everyman. My God! but the common lot, in a country like modern Italy, was a very good lot. All it required was the determination to do a little regular work. Carlo spoke about his picture as though he expected everyone to be vitally interested in it. He even attempted to explain the niceties of his method. Everyone was completely out of his or her depth. Only Lucia encouraged him. She loved to hear his excited voice and to see his arms waving about with expressive gestures. He was often so dour a man. This was like the manic side of depression. Eventually he got up to go and they all wished him goodnight, with affectionate smiles; but when he came to embrace the old man, he looked at him too directly in the eyes, a questioning look. Cesare pinched his cheek.

Carlo trudged up the long stairway. God knows what he was thinking. He probably didn't recognise the strain he had imposed on his listeners. But he was tired now. And glad when he could finally get into his bed.

That night he dreamed, dreamed of his childhood, dreams that developed into nightmares in which the jack-booted Nazi police dragged his mother away from him, and beat his father. Then he saw his Uncle Cesare conspiring with a grinning Nazi to abduct his wife, throw her into the back of a lorry with the others, all torn and bleeding. He could stand the images no more. He screamed in his bed. It was not the first time he had done so. He got up, made his way to the kitchen, blubbering like a child. He made himself some coffee, and, with his dressing gown about him, went into his studio. He switched on the lights and studied his new painting. He thought it was good, very good. Then he looked into its eyes, the eyes of the man he had painted. They were dead eyes. Yes, the eyes of Death. But it was the truth. He had painted what he had seen and painted it well.

No, the painting was not finished, but there was enough there to tell its tale. What purpose in finishing it all off? The more he did that, the more he would be distancing himself from the truth which he had, at last, uttered. "This will be my legacy!" he said aloud. And left the room.

He went into his bedroom and began to dress, putting the little velvet bag in his pocket, as if to return it to its owner. He was no longer tired despite the agony of the night. He opened his front door, walked down his path, and took the stairway down to the Pensione Garibaldi. He had a key, of course, and the guard dog knew him. Softly he made his way along the inside corridor to his uncle's room. He turned the door knob, and, as he expected, the room was not locked. His uncle lay in the bed, snoring heavily. Carlo carefully removed the prayer-shawl from its bag and held it, stretched out, over the sleeping man. "Here is my blessing," whispered Carlo; then dragged the scarf like lightening under the old man's head, before pulling it as tight as death round his wrinkled throat. The old man hadn't even time to cry out. Carlo stood over him, as though wondering why he had done it. There were tears in his eyes as he bent over the bed and kissed his uncle tenderly on the forehead. Then Carlo left the house.

He made his way slowly down to the seafront, to the Piazza IX Aprile, located at the top of an enormous cliff, covered in spring flowers, rising steeply above the sea. The grandest belvedere of the famous resort. All was clear in the brilliant moonlight. Carlo had time. The body would not be discovered yet. But he was wrong. Already a police car was racing down the snaking "boulevard". Carlo put one leg over the protecting railing. He glanced towards Etna. Yes, the fire was clear and it was growing. Let it grow! Let it engulf all Sicily! That other fire had engulfed a third of his people, six million souls, among whom his Aunt Coco, his mother, his father, his aunts, his uncles, his cousins. But his Uncle Cesare had escaped. He himself, Carlo, had escaped. He did not deserve to live! No, he did not deserve to live! The words hammered in his brain, loud as hammers striking. He heard the roar of the volcano. It was not the Etna he could see with his eyes but the Etna he could hear in his head whose burning entrails were forever exhibited on the Corso, accompanied by *The Ride of the Valkyre*. He saw the picture postcards of decayed bodies standing in stricken attitudes, as photographed in the crypt of a Palermo church. He saw the hundreds of bodies piled on carts being carted away from Auschwitz or Buchenwald or Maidanek. As he fell, he fell faster ever faster, plummeting into the abyss, his Hell on earth.

Naturally, I was cleared of all suspicion, but the house was in mourning. Nevertheless, mourning must make way for gladness on Easter morning. When it came round, the breakfast tables were decorated with flowers and Easter confectionery— hard-boiled eggs set in sweet biscuit, sprinkled with hundreds and thousands, and chocolate eggs in coloured wrappings. There was a little flower-pot on each table, with long golden wisps among, and surrounding, the blooms, like a crown: "Buona Pasqua!"

But I was ill-at-ease. It was still the Passover and I should not have been here. Those souls who fail to celebrate the Passover "shall be cut off from the congregation of Israel."

Parkin-Jewell

Clarimond Parkin-Jewel went out to Kenya, after graduating in 1936. He had taken first-class honours in Classics, but looked to the Colonies for the traditionally enterprising life his English spirit sought, at that time, as its inalienable inheritance. He had already distinguished himself as an athlete, and what with his dark good looks, there was no reason why he should not make a suitable marriage with a daughter of one of the well-established Colonial families. So he went out, in effect, as an Assistant Master at the very decent public school in Nairobi, hoping to spend his long vacations at home in England.

Taking his leave of his parents at the quayside, he smiled in his characteristically debonair manner, but underneath the smile was, as usual, the peculiar ghost of harrassment that haunted him and that made his parents anxious on his behalf. That presence never left him, whether he were diving into the swimming pool or hitting a "four" to the boundary, whether he were dancing a tango or sipping a sherry: the faintly obtrusive presence of harrassment, unease. But Clarimond Parkin-Jewell was usually its master, could usually laugh it off.

When he arrived he was warmly welcomed
by the Headmaster, at whose table, together
with the Headmaster's wife and their
eighteen-year old daughter, he dined that
evening in the very comfortable residence
fittingly allotted to such a dignitary; and
Clarimond entered at once into the spirit of
it all, talking politely but wittily, sitting
elegantly over his apéritif, and manipulating
his cutlery at dinner with poised dexterity.
Mr and Mrs Booth were decidedly impressed,
whilst Eileen took quite a fancy to the
queerly named Mr Parkin-Jewell, though she
harboured a secret ironic reserve. For she
could see, as others apparantly could not, the
little goblin of unease hovering maliciously
about his chin and finely chiselled mouth—
which caused her to say very little that
evening, though she glanced curiously from
time to time in an effort to puzzle out the
discrepancy between what appeared as his
urbanity and what spoke to her heart. She
was a tallish young woman, with a bony
frame and very round nut-brown eyes, but
with an intensity of spirit that made her
seem to quiver rather than simply breathe
and move. Clarimond took very little notice
of her, being chiefly concerned to impress her
parents, but was careful to pay her the
attention that politeness demanded. His
hosts were delighted, keeping him talking—

or rather listening—till eleven in the evening, with stories of Africa: the bush, the primitive habits of servants, the political rivalries among the Whites, the bush. Curious how, despite all their European sophistication, they kept coming back, with after all a strange gleam in their eyes, to the bush, the mysteries of it, the dangers, the weird dress and dances of the people who still dwelt there, the filth and disease. But how much more humanly satisfying it was to be sitting here, in the lounge, bathed in artificial light, upon softly cushioned armchairs, drinking brandy and smoking, than to be grubbing in that hideous green jungle, alive with shrieks and malodorous evils, that constituted the home of the benighted bush-people! Yes, Parkin-Jewell assented to this, smiling over the edge of his glass, with a little green devil of unease troubling his eyes.

He proved to be a very capable schoolmaster. Early in the morning he was to be found in class, with his long Bachelor of Arts gown swaying behind him as he scribbled on the blackboard, bits of chalk-dust settling relentlessly upon it. Then he would sit down, and, after gently smoothing the sides of his head with his sensitively clean hands, the left one bearing a bright gold ring that shone out against the oily blackness of his hair, he would turn to the class and put questions about case-endings and tenses, relating to usages of the Latin or Greek languages—the languages of civilisation. He also taught Classical History, and, with the upper classes, discussed the glories of Roman and Greek literature, betraying a taste for finely turned lyrical expression and the sentiments of pastoral love or rustic nostalgia. He was not especially well liked by the boys, but he was respected, and, all things considered, Clarimond Parkin-Jewell was well content.

He spent his first vacation making a little expedition up country. He wanted to see (naturally he did) the kind of country he was living in. So, he observed the flora and fauna; he visited several native villages; he reflected on the possiblity of further commercial exploitation; and he concerned himself with possible political ramifications. Of course, a comprehensive study could not be undertaken in the course of a single expedition, but a start could be made. Hearing of his intention, Eileen Booth boldly asked Mr Parkin-Jewell if she might accompany him. Since, to his surprise, it turned out that she had not first consulted her father, he promised to do so himself, after nevertheless explaining, in his courteously patronising way, that he thought the living conditions he expected to experience could not be suitable for an eighteen-year old girl. She realised at once that he did not want her to go—she was in fact but mischievously teasing him—so, lest he should take the matter any further, she heartily agreed, averring that she had had no idea he was planning so arduous a journey. He must promise, though, Eileen insisted, to give her a full account—and she stressed the word "full"—of all that should happen during the expedition. Clarimond rather awkwardly said he would, and watched her turn away, very decidedly, after a sudden friendly wave, to walk down the little path leading from his front door to the private road that served the school estate. He walked slowly back into his house, the look of harrassment more pronouncedly on his features than ever. But he could not say what troubled him. All he knew was that the girl had made him feel both silly and clumsy—two characteristics he did not usually associate with himself. He shrugged his shoulders and got on with making preparations for his expedition up country.

The effect of the jungle on Clarimond was not unlike the effect of Eileen Booth on him. It left him uneasy, puzzled, rather blank. Though he was a man with a curious, alert mind, he found that he soon grew somewhat bored by the jungle. Perhaps there was so much there that it bewildered the senses and left the mind blank. Nor did he see much to interest or disturb him in the village communities he managed to glimpse. To his surprise, he saw relatively ordinary people performing their daily chores: cooking, washing clothes, mending huts, making tools or weapons for hunting—laughing, gossiping, quarrelling sometimes. The only difference between the jungle people (as he pleased to call them) and the people of Surbiton, Surrey, seemed to be in the colour of their skin, the shape of their features, the kind of clothes they wore, their language, and—the one thing which did impress Clarimond—the occasional signs of hideous disease. But even these could be seen in the local Surbiton Hospital; so why let it over-concern one? No, Clarimond, to his surprise, came back from his first holiday-excursion with the, for him, surprising conclusion that all men were alike, that the human family was one indeed. This wasn't idealism on his part, but the product of a habit of observation made in a spirit of impersonal enquiry, which he had acquired during his time as an undergraduate studying Classics at Cambridge. He was a civilised man looking at Africa and he found Africa relatively civilised. Why fuss? The only disappointment in this discovery was the boredom which was its consequence. He might almost as well have taken a trip up the Thames from near Surbiton. When he kept his promise to Eileen, on getting back to Nairobi, and told her all that had happened to him, and consequently of his disappointment, she laughed and laughed. But he begged her not to tell anyone what he had said, because he felt it incumbent upon him to embroider the account somewhat for the benefit of other people. He had found himself making a confidant, then, of Eileen, but was grateful, as well as surprised and slightly uneasy, that he had done so. He didn't thereupon go telling wild stories of his trip to other acquaintances who asked him about it, or to those to whom he felt obliged to say something even unasked, but he tended to highlight the few outstanding incidents and play down the prevailing boredom, which was the real outcome of the expedition. Next vacation he would return to England to see his parents.

Once back in England, he really wondered whether he wanted to go back to Africa. He found the English climate so pleasant in its mildness and the English people so agreeable in their native setting—and since, belonging to a privileged class he had no need to encounter the sordid side of English life (the barbaric side, as you might say)—he

wondered whether he really at any rate
ought not to renew his contract, when it
came up for review in the following year.
With that rather comforting thought in
mind, he had the incentive to enjoy the rest
of his English holiday and go back bravely,
feeling the door to freedom stood, as it were,
ever ajar; but something was drawing him to
Africa nevertheless. His thought about
contracts was merely an unconscious excuse.
He wanted to go back but didn't want the
responsibility of owning the fact. He didn't
want to know that something was drawing
him, against his English taste for the commonplace (which after all so many English men
and women have resisted), back to Africa.
The look of unease, however, was less often
on his face as his fate was deciding itself
beyond his conscious will. He went back, then,
gaily this time. His parents were beginning to
wonder what had come over him.

The routine of the school soon made
Clarimond its own once again. He was the
epitome of correct behaviour: punctual in
class and at meals, impeccably fair as referee
or umpire, polite in social intercourse with
the families of other staff, amusing sometimes
in the commonroom (in a dry, ironic sort of
way), always ready to oblige and cooperate
—in fact, just a little, something of a toady.
But, nevertheless, he was so capable a man,

so knowledgeable about his subject, so generally well informed, and (as we have noted) so polite and helpful, that he escaped with only the occasional whisper of ill-will against him, which, in any case, could easily be ascribed to the jealousy of a rival. The Headmaster was particularly predisposed towards him, but certainly didn't favour him unfairly. No one, in fact, had any real grounds for complaint; and Clarimond was just a bit smug on that account. The Headmaster's daughter he had begun to take just a little more notice of, but, characteristically of her sex, she seemed inclined to ignore him. Clarimond was too complacent to be much hurt, but he was irritated. He thought he must pay her the same compliment. Eileen seemed to want nothing better! And so Clarimond Parkin-Jewell lived quite fully up to the suggestion of his name: he was faintly patronising or supercilious, but perfectly correct and gentlemanly. If only he had been the proprietor of a prosperous farm, or, at least, the Headmaster of a prestigious school, the correspondence between name and station would have been perfect; yet Mr Booth was not disinclined to think of him as a prospective son-in-law.

But the sun was hot, damnably hot, and a man had to muster all his resources to keep his composure, to stop the sweat that broke out all over his body from invading, as it were, the cool recesses of his mind, and to stop the thoughts, that seemed to be nourished by the heavy air of the jungle, from driving out purer thoughts inspired by the civilised works of Greek and Roman literature. A man had to fight for his status as a European out here, fight against himself even, and this made the achievement, the victory of his good sense, the more meritorious. For it wasn't simply the physical, but the metaphysical, struggle that had to be undertaken; and the more intelligent he was the more vulnerable a man might be—if that intelligence was of the kind that led him to explore the nature of his own consciousness, such as a persistent frequentation of imaginative literature was likely to be. So, never was Clarimond's suit anything but well pressed, and never was his face anything but smoothly shaved. Never did he lose control of his temper—never did he neglect the smallest duty of an English gentleman abroad. But, if he grew more confident of keeping at bay the menace of the African jungle, he remained uneasy about his relationship with Eileen Booth. She remained an unknown quantity, and a disturbingly magnetic one. Was she, in some sense, as compulsive a reality for him as Africa itself?

Once again he had to decide how to spend his vacation, and, again, he decided to venture into the interior, this time in company with a colleague with whom he had grown friendly —Justin Fairfax. Justin was as fair-haired as his name might suggest, if not, in character, as just. That is to say, he had an appetite for exploring the seedier side of life. He was to be found in dubious nightclubs, consorting with shady characters, women of easy virtue, black and white; he gambled, he drank. He was a man who had plunged into the depths of himself: a more real element than any external environment could be, whether of desert or jungle. He was not that kind of explorer. Ostensibly, he was a teacher of school Geography; and whatever rumours might circulate about him, you couldn't ask a man to resign because of them. Besides, Mr Booth thought him professionally very competent. Here, then, was another challenge for Clarimond. First, it was the "evils" of the jungle; now, it was the dissipations of the city. Not that he intended to draw any nearer to them than he did in drawing nearer to Justin himself; but all was suggestion to Clarimond—what he might learn and experience thus vicariously. He knew that his soul was in just as much danger, perhaps more.

And the more he thought about it, the more did the old truth impress itself upon

him: that life was indubitably constituted of
the dark and the light, the corrupt and the
pure. There was God and there was the
Devil; there was good and there was evil.
The problem was to discern the one from the
other, and then have the strength either to
elect oneself a denizen of darkness, or
(perhaps the harder choice) to confess a
preference for the light. Most souls seemed
to leave the matter to chance.

After all, the ancient literature of patriotic
or romantic love was counterbalanced by
that of dissipation, cruel satire, the exposure
of hideous vices like sores on the face of
humanity.

But it was Justin, not Clarimond, who was
bewitched by the jungle. He did not see only
human beings engaged in their daily round of
menial business, something analogous after
all to the routine of the school back in
Nairobi: the little movements and gestures
that keep civilisation alive, that make a
pattern out of the incoherent sum of events.
He saw the sinister world that legend speaks
of—the devil-possessed Continent alive with
evils too hideous to specify, a terrified
humanity in thrall to malicious metaphysical
powers, a festering mire of disease and
infamy. By night, most of all, did he love the
jungle—the deathly stillness torn by shrieks
of unseen animals; scufflings in the branches;

gleams of starlight above the canopy formed by foliage of gigantic trees. And the sound of drums. The jungle was, for Justin Fairfax, alive with death, in shadow, screeching, moving incessantly, disease-ridden. But Clarimond failed to respond. Only in Nairobi, back in the comfort of the school, could he feel all this, was he in thrall to it. Here, in its heart, he was the Surbiton Englishman, contemptuous, indifferent. Books, perhaps, were more important to him than life, un-reality than reality, suggestion than fact. All he could do here was think of Surbiton, whilst his friend lay enchanted with horror on his mosquito-netted bunk. Clarimond fixed his eyes, once again, on his book, yawned, and went on reading. It was *The History of Mr Polly*.

"And how did you like it this time?" said Eileen, (when, with relief, he got back) arching her beautiful nut-brown eyes, which were queerly round like an owl's. Clarimond didn't answer at first. He was removing some dirty tea cups from the little table—his "boy" was out at the time—and he made her wait till he had finished. Then he smiled and said, very quietly:

"Mr Faifax is the romantic, I'm afraid, Miss Booth. Not I."

He smiled again.

She laughed.

"You mean it's all just Surbiton again?"

"Exactly. Won't you let me make you a cup of coffee? I do find that the one vice Kenya has developed in me is an addiction to the domestic stimulants—tannin and cafein. I don't mind which."

She looked at him rather severely.

"Well, if you must accentuate your English habits out here, I suppose you must," she said. "But remember, I'm an African."

He laughed. He could never get over this, as he thought, queer insistence of hers, that she was an African. Of course, she had been born in Kenya, just as her mother had, but that this made her an African in any but the most trivial sense Clarimond could not accept, and it puzzled him that she should keep insisting (as she did), with a kind of contempt for him (he thought). An African, for him, was necessarily a black man, or woman, not a genteel English rose transplanted to African soil.

"Well," he said, "if you're an African, I'm a Dutchman!"

And he laughed again, as he rose to put the coffee on.

"But you're more an African than I am," he heard her say, calling from the sitting room.

For some reason, his skin crept at the words, but he composed his face and, smiling

as he re-entered the room, he said that the
only kind of African he was, was a China-clay
African. Something that might look like an
African to those who had rather poor
taste—he said, looking at her cheekily—but
which was nothing but air inside and an
artificial glaze on the front. It fell to pieces if
you dropped it and it was probably made in
Surbiton!

They chuckled together over his rather
successful witticism, but he wasn't comfortable. He knew there was truth in her words.

"Well, if you're not an African," she went
on, with a rather foolish persistence, "at least
I am."

"Sugar?" he said, offering her the basin.

She took two lumps.

"And how did *you* spend the vacation?" he
inquired politely, not caring.

"I went up to my grandpa's. We always do
at this time of the year."

He knew that her grandparents still ran a
prosperous farm in the highlands.

"And did anything exciting happen to
you?" he asked, remembering his own
vacational disappointment.

"How do you mean? Did I see any lions?
Was I harrassed by jackals? Well yes, I was in
a way. I got engaged!"

She looked at him very steadily as she said
this, with a perfectly serious expression. He

half rose in his chair, staring at her. Her face twitched a little. Then he sat down again, smiling suavely.

"And I," he said, "became the husband of an African chieftainess."

"But I did get engaged," she repeated. "Really. I haven't got a ring yet, because it isn't official—and I don't want you to tell anyone. But I got engaged to a very distant relative of ours. It isn't incestuous, though." She hesitated. "He's called Peter Carstairs, and he works for the Broadcasting Corporation in London."

Clarimond now believed her. His smile slipped away and it was replaced by the little goblin of unease that hadn't been seen on his face for a very long time. He was about to utter his correct congratulations when he saw that she had tricked him. This time he could not control his appearance and he blushed awkwardly, awkwardly and angrily, as she laughed uncontrollably for a few moments.

"Well," she said, taking pity on him, " you shouldn't tease me about being an African. And there, you see, I've proved it—by being as treacherous as the jungle. Can I have a biscuit?"

He offered her the little, flowered plate, pursing his lips in relieved and mock astonishment, looking very openly into her round, merry, nut-brown eyes.

"Your father should teach you not to trifle with a gentleman's feelings," he said quickly.

"Didn't know you had any!" she replied with equal rapidity, busying herself with the half-eaten biscuit. "Good heavens! Half past three! I'm supposed to be going into town with Mummy this afternoon. Do you mind? I must just swallow this mouthful, and then—"

She had already got up, and, replacing her empty cup, askew on its saucer, she smiled briefly at Mr Parkin-Jewell, and waved him goodbye as she fled down the path.

On his second English vacation, in 1938, Clarimond felt sure that war in Europe was near. But, as we know, the outbreak was delayed. He returned to Africa and his now more senior post at the school, whilst Eileen travelled with her mother, for sixth months, through Britain, France, Germany, Italy, and Greece. But whatever noises—of printing presses, radio broadcasts, and indeed even of the movement of armies—heralded the destinies of the European nations at this time, in the heart of the jungle only the calls of beasts could be heard and the rustling of superabundant vegetation. Justin Fairfax had by now given notice to terminate his employment at the school, having aquired a grant to explore a remote river basin. News of him came rarely, but Clarimond followed it

with the keenest interest. As for himself, he
continued teaching, doggedly, irreproachably,
dutifully—a pillar of the school establishment.
In fact, at the end of the year he was made
Housemaster on the retirement of Mr
Foldes. 1939 saw the maintenance of the old
routine at the school, until shortly before the
Declaration of War. Parkin-Jewell took his
leave of the Headmaster, Mrs Booth, and
Eileen, as of the rest of the school personnel,
arriving in England in time to volunteer for
the R.A.F. just before hostilities began.

He was employed in aerial reconnaisance,
flying over enemy territory to take photographs of possible bombing targets. This was
as enjoyable a time as he had ever spent. The
danger and the altitude filled him with a sort
of perpetual light intoxication. His keen eyes
observed the contours of the land below
him—a peaceful activity except for the
heavy drone of the aircraft's engines. He
watched the green fade into brown as the
lowlands gave way to highlands, then
mountains that reached up to the clouds
through which the aircraft was intermittently
flying. Over the gently undulating green land
of England, over the grey sea, the white cliffs
of Normandy, over the woods and plains of
northern France, into the Vosges mountains,
within range of the Alps. At night, he saw
below him flashes of artillery fire, as he

sought to identify the movement of convoys creeping along with dimmed lights, whilst his aircraft flew steadily on through the inky blackness lit faintly by drifting masses of grey cloud and points of starlight above and around—until, on one occasion, a shell burst against the fuselage of his 'plane and he landed, by parachute, in enemy territory.

He was found, wounded, by Resistance fighters, who hid him and secured medical treatment for him; he was passed from safe-house to safe-house, until he was well enough to take part in sabotage activities. Here he came into his own, initiating moves, planning the campaign. And here he remained, behind enemy lines, for the rest of the war—a Special Operations officer who was now in touch by clandestine radio with British Intelligence.

He had been intoxicated by action, bold action, so that return to a peaceful existence, after the defeat of Fascism and Nazism, was anathema to him. He walked the London streets, in a time of austerity, with bomb-sites still disfiguring them, yet the enormous relief felt by most people, despite their war-weariness, he did not share. It was as though the glamour of life had faded for him—had faded with the spilt blood, the roar of artillery, the whining of dive-bombers: the great drama of life and death, in which the

fate of nations was involved. He knew this
way of thinking was wicked, but he could
not help himself. But his father, whose soul
had been scarred by action in the first of the
two world wars, seemed to understand. So
there was no protest when Clarimond spoke
of returning to Africa, even if he declared
himself averse to schoolteaching. No, he
would go to Kenya and see what he could
find. What he hoped to find was Eileen, and
perhaps Justin Fairfax.

He was heavier in build, more lined in the
face, more determined, more mature than he
had been in 1936, when he went out to
Africa for the first time, with the little goblin
of dissatisfaction playing about his chin and
mouth. The presence had now become a
demon that lived in the depths of his heart
and it was demanding the propitiation which
life owed it in the person of Clarimond
Parkin-Jewell.

He found Eileen working as a nurse in the
Hospital at Nairobi, and he asked her if she
would consent to accompany him on a long-
delayed excursion into the bush, to seek the
whereabouts of Justin Fairfax who had not
been heard of for years. She said she would go.

He did not scorn the jungle now. He
entered it as he would a temple. His eyes
were wide with wonder, his whole body being
inundated by the sights and sounds and

scents of this vast unknowable region, in
whose depths still lived remnants of his
fellow man, though (it now seemed to him)
they were of strange habits and strange
ways. But he thought they might show him a
way back into his own soul, which had been
emasculated by that complexity of formulae
which constituted the English way of life—
at any rate, the life of his class and kindred.
What more there was could easily be seen in
the tragic plays of Sophocles and Æschylus,
which had begun to displace, in his mental
library, those more graceful works he had
once preferred. But now it was the more
concrete experience that called—the
progress by canoe along the endless river,
overhung by creepers, an artery of the jungle.

They made various stops, for information
and provisions, at riverside villages. But never
a word of Fairfax. Ten years in fact was more
than the native people could be made to
understand. Ten years was before the Flood
perhaps. Certainly it was beyond the memory
of all but the oldest men, and they had news
only of supernatural occurences associated
with their youth, news that they relayed in
poetical paeans of infinite duration and in a
dialect that was impossible to understand.
But Clarimond began to listen more keenly
to these mysteries the more he left the
enlightened world behind. He was listening

to the rhythms of the language, the sonorities of the syllables, and watching the expressions of the old men's faces as they warmed and saddened to their mysterious tales. He thought he was beginning to understand their meaning at last: it was the story of mankind; and as the realisation—valid or not in terms of literal interpretation—dawned, a great outpouring of love towards these wizened human beings, chanting in high broken voices, came from him. When they wept, at the account of some tragic event, he wept too, though he had no idea of the literal meaning of those words, and when they were joyful he was joyful too, without artifice, without thought. He might have been listening to a great music.

And as she watched him, Eileen began to feel love for this strange man, just as he loved the tellers of incomprehensible tales, and they loved him for listening to and "understanding" them. Gazing at him, she noticed with pleasure and surprise that the little goblin of unease was exorcised at last.

There was no need to look further for Justin Fairfax. His essence had disappeared, perhaps into the heart of Africa itself. To find him was to listen to these old men. But they were dying now. Not only them but the world from which they came—the ancient

past of humanity. The white blight was
spreading through all the untouched places
of the earth, till one deadly disease alone
could speak for our humanity. For the sons of
Africa must follow where we have led.

They journeyed on, alone, into the
darkness, without hope. They did not speak
and did not take care for provisions. But they
journeyed. The jungle never changed. The
river widened or narrowed, but never
changed. The water was the water, and the
jungle the jungle. On into the interior. Into
the heart. Their canoe drifted into a wide
expanse of water, a lake, with a straggle of
dwellings by the bank. Here they learned
that Faifax had drifted there before them,
years ago, and had died of fever. His body had
been committed to the lake. Clarimond and
Eileen paid their respects to his spirit, and
set off for home, not really expecting to
reach it.

But "Civilisation Saves!" Into the clearing
one fine day a helicopter flew, the crew
looking for missing persons. Clarimond and
Eileen were picked up soon after, albeit by
then more dead than alive. And so, they were
thrown back helplessly into the maelstrom of
civilised life. They felt humiliated and were
bewildered. Almost desultorily they decided
to marry and to go to England. And so, he
became a schoolmaster again; and she

evidenced a certain silly coquettishness as she ministered to the wives of his colleagues at the tea-table: for he had found a position in a very prestigious public school, in Surrey. His health, however, was broken. There he was, though, at the master's desk, smoothing his still black hair, with the little gold ring shining on his left hand (now partnered by a grander wedding ring on his fourth finger), clearing his throat, and telling of Greece and Rome; whilst she, a bold upstanding woman with a rather brown skin, and beautiful nut-brown eyes so round, told tales of Africa, at the tea table, in a not very striking way— stories of servants doing stupid things, and of the bush, and of Nairobi, but never of their journey up the river towards life. And he, likewise, never spoke of their journey to anyone, until neither of them, when they thought of it, could decide whether it had been reality or dream. But the river knew the answer to that question.

Pont St Esprit

As the car came round the last bend on to
the bridge, he was there in the headlights —
a solitary figure, tapping with a cane, a black
cloth covering his face. The occupants of the
car shuddered, the driver staring ahead to
avoid a fatal distraction. Uncannily the yellow
beams emphasised the strange darkness of
the figure, caught against the low grey
parapet of the bridge with the unseen water
below. He must have been in middle-age,
judging by the stout dignity of his frame and
his measured pace to God-knows-where. But
there was no knowing more, for, in an
instant, they were past and speeding on into
the night, into the dry *garrigues*, the stony
heathland of southern France.

It was an ancient bridge, where pilgrims had
walked, and below, when sunlight glinted upon
it, the waters of the Rhône ran peacefully,
carrying barges down to Avignon, to Marseille;
and the ancient stone houses huddled around
the church whose roof shone green. Now the
streets, shaded by the foliage of plane-trees,
were filled with motor cars and well-dressed
people. In the evening they were vibrant with
the chatter and clatter of busy cafés.

Beyond lay the vineyards, the outcrops of
white limestone, silence, and the haunts of

other forms of life. The terrified eyes of a fox might stare back through the headlamp beams of a speeding car.

Three times it had appeared to them (like Hamlet's ghost) at the same spot, at the same time. And still their blood ran cold. Yet the tapping of the cane was not fearsome, simply practical. They were not the steps of a madman, rather of a blind man. But why the elaborate outfit, complete with hat, as though, perhaps, he were deliberately trying to frighten people? A sardonic phantom.

So, as they raced on into the *garrigues*, behind them still was the man with the veiled face, walking over the bridge which carries traffic into the Midi—Roussillon and Languedoc. Alone in the darkness, tapping his cane, seemingly oblivious of the glaring headlamps, the curiosity or fear of unseen eyes. Unseen as water below the bridge, lapping in the moonlight. And he was walking against the flow of the traffic, on the near side, passing the vehicles within inches on his right. Impossible to know if he detected their presence, yet carefully keeping to the narrow pavement, looking neither to left nor right, neither up nor down, but straight on, against the flow of the traffic, into the night on the other side, as a witch murmuring her incantations backward. Contrary to the flow. Widdershins.

Mademoiselle Paul

The heavy wooden doors, laced with metal, fitted into ancient stonework and opened on to a gloomy passage at the end of which snarled a mahogany griffin mounted on a pedestal, which beast guarded an ornamental lamp which remained lighted for three minutes at a time. Wide stone stairs led to an elaborately fashioned doorway, bearing a doctor's nameplate, by which stood vases of tropical plants; then, making a left right-angle turn, the stairs led up beneath the skylight to the double doors which marked the confines of Mademoiselle Paul's spacious flat.

She greeted you with the sound of hurrying heels on wood, flung open the door and ushered you into a rather elegantly furnished room dominated by a large grand piano in its walnut case. There was a lamp angle-poised over the music stand, shedding light on to a score, and, standing with its back square to one of the room's corners, was a glass-fronted show-case displaying a variety of miniature ornaments, together with one or two heavy encyclopaedias.

She was a woman of middle height, good figure, and a noticeably straight back, wearing spectacles tinted to counteract the strong Mediterranean glare, her medium-length hair being as dark as you would expect of a southern Frenchwoman.

She spoke in a rapid, breathless manner, switching from one tone to another and flitting from one subject to the next, whilst she fixed you with a steady gaze either from behind the two dark lenses or—but only occasionally—without their intervention, from a pair of nut-brown eyes, one of them slightly a-squint.

She was perhaps in her early thirties and taught music in the Conservatoire, specifically the piano.

Each day she walked quickly along the streets, in her straight skirt and high-heeled shoes, with a handbag slung from her shoulder, past the flower-stalls in front of the fish-market, and across the square lined with the carts of costermongers. She seemed to be blind and deaf to her surroundings, concealed behind her tinted lenses, walking swiftly, dressed usually in black, like a shadow, till she came to the Conservatoire whose broad-arched entry gave on to an ancient street. Once inside the courtyard, the sound of musical instruments could be heard, emanating from the various practice-rooms overlooking it. Mademoiselle Paul mounted to the first floor of the building, and, after registering her presence by an exchange of routine greetings with the male secretary (who was also a music teacher, a trumpeter), she entered her classroom.

Here she taught with enthusiasm, with energy, with inspiration. She sang phrases from the piano-scores—Beethoven, Chopin, greater and lesser composers of the French school, Bach—tapped out rhythms, demonstrated her meaning at the instrument: she cajoled, remonstrated, praised, gave vent to anger, exasperation. Her being was wholly given over to music and to the teaching of it; so that, at the end of her day, she was exhausted.

She would return to her flat and, in summer, then make her way to a nearby beach. There she would change into her swimming costume and cast herself into the waves—to swim mindlessly, working her limbs as they were never worked in the classroom, shabby with years of use, shutting out the sun, the air stale by comparison with that which came off the sea, dusty despite whatever cleaning it submitted to.

Sometimes a pupil would carry the memory of her in her mind forever. Not only the instruction she gave but the person who gave it—the sound of her voice, her mannerisms: such as her sitting with crossed legs, adjusting her garments as she spoke; or rubbing her eyes with one hand while the

other held her spectacles; or the occasion
when, in the midst of a torrent of words,
cascading from her lips, she suddenly tossed
up her outer skirt almost to her face, like an
excited child. Such a pupil might remember
her generosity too, giving a fellow pupil
money to buy himself a decent lunch,
because he would not otherwise be able to
afford one, refusing to accept payment for
extra tuition from another pupil because she
perceived such payment might entail
hardship.

But it was at her *auditions* that she was in
her element. Here she played host to a dozen
pupils and their parents in her flat, so that
they might be heard by her own former
teacher, now the Director of an important
Conservatoire in another town, who came
with his wife to Mademoiselle Paul's flat too.
The table was laid in the grandest style, to
be approached only at the end of the session,
which was long and uncompromisingly
serious—a series of recitals of set-pieces by
Mademoiselle Paul's pupils, punctiliously and,
sometimes, it must be said, even cruelly
(despite Madame's protestations to which
her husband would not listen) criticised,
constructively of course, by the Master. To
the better pupils such an occasion was a
revelation and a privilege, an occasion when
ears even more experienced, much more

experienced, than even those of the admirable Mademoiselle Paul, were at the service of their humble efforts, efforts which the Master might, on rare occasions, find excitingly promising, so that his own enthusiasm would burn bright.

A foreign student was once the subject of such enthusiasm. The Master drove her, harder and harder, to achieve the effects he wanted, and they coincided with those she wanted, so she strove the more willingly, finding in herself resources of which she had previously been unaware. The music was in the "modern" vein: that is to say, it had been composed in the earlier years of the twentieth century, and it was French in origin. The performance of it required very great "technical" skill in the playing and "balancing" of chords as well as in contrapuntal articulation and in the execution of the expressive andante sections, the work being, besides, massive in scale—a manifest challenge to the musician in a pianist as well as the virtuoso.

The Master was exultant and the pupil thrilled to her inner being. Here was the joy of living, the joy of music, the joy of learning. Nothing else mattered. For these few moments the price of a whole lifetime was worth paying. She would know no intenser joy than this—no, not if a theatre echoed with the applause of a full house in acknowledgement of her performance; and, if it did, she would know the seeds of it were sown here, in an apartment overlooking a lamplit square, where the foliage of plane-trees was loud with the clamour of birds, on a warm Mediterranean evening.

Don Juan and the Goats

She threw herself at him and he caught her. He loved the way she pronounced his name and she pronounced it constantly. He loved her big brown eyes, for she had big brown eyes. And he coveted her lithe young body. Ah, to feel that living body pressing against his own! Ah, Paradise! Paradise that is a woman's body melting under one's touch, so that flesh becomes a deliquescence, a throb in the night!

But there was his wife—so solid in her domesticity, amidst children and cabbages and goats, in a dirty pinafore. Oh why, when all the novels and plays and poems in the world spoke of love and its ambrosial sweetness, must he be fastened to a dirty apron? He would snap the strings, with the finality of a fling for Life!

To look at him you would never guess the maelstrom of romantic feelings within him. He was rather short, sturdy in body, and curly-haired; and he walked with his head thrust backward from straight shoulders, with a short neck. Though his eyes were extraordinarily deep-set and blue, he wore big intellectual spectacles, for he was an intellectual. Yes, he discussed books, novels which had a pessimistic slant, which spoke of the inner corruption of ambitious men; and he liked to fancy himself compassionate, broad-minded, humble. Some women found him very attractive.

Lucinda was an extrovert. She breezed through life with the confidence of a fallen angel. She knew she could wind men round her little finger, and she was going to do it, for her own sake and for the sake of women in general—the oppressed sex. Not that Derek was simply her victim. No, she had a passion for him. Anyway, Derek eventually, gradually, became her lover.

After all, wasn't it Paradise he was being offered, on a plate? Who could refuse the offer but a cold-hearted Angelo? And he was no Angelo. No, he was an eager consumer of Life's bounties. No hypocrite he. What, "exercise restraint" and, as a consequence, be fed upon by all sorts of unhealthy desires? Be in the lists with Satan every day, taking the blows and rarely, so rarely, being able to return one? No, not he. Had he not learned, even from the writings of that uneven genius D. H. Lawrence, that desire was paramount?

No, he decided that that which bound him to his wife was a mere form, a false bond which must be broken. Besides, he thought, "Am I not now living a novel, and isn't that worlds better than merely reading or even writing one? Isn't Life to be preferred to Art?" So, in a way, he felt he was, essentially, on the side of the angels.

Yet he was not happy to see the sufferings of his wife, poor Barbara; and he was not happy in deceiving her. When it all came out there were dreadful scenes. But this, too, was Life, wasn't it? Oh, if the heart and soul could withstand such storms, how much wiser and deeper would the heart and soul become!

What puzzled him was the indifference of his goats. Now that was silly, obviously. The goats weren't to know anything, but they suggested a queer continuity in his life. There they were—bleating, nibbling, pissing, gazing peaceably about the world. While the world spun and shook; while the heavens whirled round vertiginously; while Derek's heart was breaking, then bursting with happiness, then breaking again; while the tears poured down Barbara's cheeks; while Lucinda was whispering words of love—the goats, the damned goats, went on chewing and pissing and gazing indifferently!

Tamar[*]

She sat at the roadside, on the outskirts of Ena'im, where she knew travellers bound for the sheepshearing festivities had to pass. She was dressed as a Canaanite whore, a votive of Astarte. But her heart was in mourning. Onan, her second husband, was three years dead, and the boy she had been promised, his brother Shelah, though now of marrying age, had been withheld from her. She was angry as well as sad, and, as a vigorous young woman still, she was frustrated of her natural desires—for had not her father-in-law expressly forbidden her to marry another? How indeed was she to bear children, as her nature as well as the expectations of her own father and those of her tribe demanded that she should? She sat in the shade of a tree, but the heat of the day was intense, so that she perspired uncomfortably beneath her gaudy robes and the veil covering her face. The sound of sheep was everywhere, and the spectacle of shepherds herding them along the road and across the open land towards Ena'im, on the way to their ultimate destination of Timnah, where the celebrations would be held—a wild, frenzied commotion of sheep-shearing, drinking, bonfires, dancing,

[*] Genesis xxxviii

sacrifice and fornication. Judah would be
there, to enjoy the satiation of his senses as
well as to profit from his abundant flocks of
distinctively brown-fleeced animals, which
they said were the descendants of a flock his
father Jacob had acquired as the result of a
somewhat shady deal with Laban, his father-
in-law. How Judah reconciled his strange
belief in an invisible god who, apparently, set
at nought all other gods (to an extent which
many people found offensive) with a
willingness to take part in so-called "pagan"
festivals was an enigma; but perhaps it was a
policy dictated by commercial necessity, as
much as natural weakness and a sensual
nature. At any rate, this queer belief had
served his family well: for there were twelve
sons born to Jacob his father, a man who had
prospered otherwise, too. Perhaps Hirah,
Judah's Adullamite friend, might know.

It seemed that she was fated for
misfortune, mused Tamar as she watched the
slow-moving herds, pouring like sluggish
water over the undulating land. If only she
had never had anything to do with this half-
Hebrew, half-Canaanite family! Now Shua's
daughter, her mother-in-law, a Canaanite like
herself, was dead; and her father-in-law had
deceived her, keeping her dangling on a
thread, whilst Shelah to whom she was
promised was perhaps going to marry

someone else. It was all very well, but a
woman needed security in this harsh world,
and her in-laws were at least prosperous
people. Besides, she felt that, though doomed
to misfortune, there was a necessity in her
fate which perhaps was for the best. But it
had been hard, hard. First Er had died,
Judah's eldest son, to whom she had first been
given. He had beaten her, he drank heavily, he
flaunted his lust for other women before her
face, he constantly quarrelled with his father
which put an intolerable strain on ordinary
domestic relations, and he squandered his
father's substance. It was almost a blessing
that he had died. Judah, though stricken with
grief, considered it a judgement from Heaven.
She would keep an open mind about that,
but, when you had lived on terms of close
intimacy with someone, someone you did not
altogether hate, for all their misdemeanours,
you felt the wrench when they were torn
from you. But she then was given to Onan, as
custom dictated, so that he could "raise up
seed to his brother". What a fiasco and more
than fiasco that had been! Onan did not want
to raise up such seed. He rebelled against the
custom; for he did not want any son of his
own being considered a son of his dead
brother (as the first-born would be), and then
inheriting all his brother's property. Onan
would not abide by such a custom. He had

never had any love for Er. In fact, he had always
despised him, being himself a quiet man on
the whole, not a loud-mouthed swaggerer.
But he was determined, whether people mis-
took his mildness for malleability or not. She,
Tamar, would never forget her surprise when,
on the wedding night, just as she reached her
sexual climax, which seemed, miraculously, to
occur at exactly the same moment as Onan's
did, she felt him withdraw from her body and
felt the semen spurt on to her trembling leg.
She had clasped him desperately to herself,
but it was too late. The "precious
substance" was spilled. He lay there panting
but triumphant. She felt as though she could
have killed him. But that was not the worst.
It went on like that night after night. "What
are you doing to me?" she demanded in a
voice which sounded more like a plea.
"Nothing!" he jeered. "I'm doing nothing."
"But why?" She could never forget the look
of malice that came upon his features. "By
this means," he said between gritted teeth,
"I torture the soul of my brother." God
knows what else had been between them,
between the "gentle" Onan and brutal Er,
but it must have been more than the
venerable and charitable custom. However it
was, Onan died too, within a short while; and
again Judah attributed it to the Lord as
punishment for the "sin" of Onan's spilling

his precious seed on the ground: for indeed she had told her mother-in-law about the strange proceedings, and she had passed the information on to her husband. Well, now it was Shelah's turn to marry her, but Judah delayed. Why? "Because," someone had whispered, "for all his pious attribution of his sons' deaths to the Lord, he actually thinks you had something to do with it!" Well, if he thought that, his piety was false: it was on a par with his tolerance of such heathen practices as the sheep-shearing festivities. But she would have her way, she assured herself, as she readjusted her gorgeous vestments in the heat of the day, in the shade of a tree, just outside Ena'im.

"How much, my lady," came a voice in whose tone she could not distinguish between respect and irony, "for your estimable favours?"

Through her thick veil she saw little more than the silhouette of a powerful body which was stooping solicitously towards her. The man's long-legged cur was sniffing at the hem of her robe which she twitched away as he roared abuse at the animal, delivering a hefty kick at the same time. As though the incident had not occured, in a gentle voice the man again inquired about her price.

"My price is beyond your means," she replied in a low voice.

"How do you know what my means are?" he said, laughing.

The sheep baa-ed in the vast landscape, the sun beat down. Rising to her feet and stretching her two arms wide as she looked towards the open land, Tamar declared firmly, "My price is everything beneath the sky that you can see!"

"A madwoman," the man muttered as he hurried away.

She was left alone with her thoughts once again. It had been like this ever since sunrise, men pestering her, and she was growing uneasy, for word might get about that there was something suspicious about this particular votary who was not plying her authorised trade. If only Judah would come soon!

"How much, my lady?" A man of just under medium height, his right hand resting on his waist and the end of his shepherd's crook, which he held in his left, resting on the ground, stood before her. She did not like his demeanour, somehow. Involuntarily she shuddered in his presence and fleetingly wondered how truly professional whores coped with such feelings.

"How much?" he said again, impatient.

"I . . . I am about to retire from the heat of the day," she said.

"Good. I shall retire with you. Where do we go?"

"No. I mean, I am no longer at service. Not till later."

"I can't wait till 'later'. How much?" he reiterated with loud emphasis.

"The price of your soul," she said quietly.

He grabbed her by the arm, forcing her up to her feet. "Come on," he said, "I have no more time to waste."

But she would not acquiesce. "Leave me! Leave me go!" she cried. "How dare you handle a votary like this? You will be punished!"

"By whom? By an ineffable spirit?" he jeered. "Good. I'll take on as many spirits as you like—"

But two men broke away from a small group that was passing and dragged the fellow off her, bundling him away with a few slaps and kicks. "Ply your trade, lady," said one of them, "though it's a dangerous one."

Considerably ruffled, Tamar sat herself down again but could not prevent a few tears moistening her cheeks. It was much quieter now though, the bulk of the shepherds seemingly having passed on to Timnah, but there were still a few droves approaching. The vastness of land and sky began to affect her strangely, and the silence made all the more manifest by the piteous cry of distant sheep. The few dwellings that constituted Ena'im, beyond which she had stationed her

seat, were like careful piles of stones con-
structed by weak fearful creatures as protection
from the stupendous forces contained in the
illimitable universe. No mighty storm was
needed to impress upon her the littleness of
humankind: she had but to look into the
distance, where the few frail flocks nodded
their halting way forward, towards her. They
were heading for the shearing, as ignorant of
their destiny as she was of hers. But there
were gods, gods who dwelt in the universal
forces, gods in whose honour the festivities
at Timnah were to take place. Gods no one
had ever seen though, except in the form of
images which had to be revered as
representatives of the gods, images the
desecration of which would incur the anger
of the gods, images, consequently, which
people treated as being virtually the gods
themselves, images made by human beings
out of clay and wood and stone. But the
Hebrews despised such images. Jacob had
ordered his family to give up all such that
they possessed, even down to the charms
they wore as earrings, and to "purify" themselves, even changing their clothes; and it
was said that an ancestor of Judah had
actually smashed a whole quantity of holy
images, yet lived to tell the tale. It was, it
seemed to her, more reasonable, really, not to
imagine you knew what the gods looked like,

but to honour them as invisible entities.
Perhaps they despised image-making? Yet
how could they, if they knew that those who
made them and those who worshipped them
did so with sincerity and purity of heart?
Perhaps it was nevertheless the destiny of
Israel (which was what his sons mysteriously
called their father Jacob) to oppose that
natural out-come of pious feeling in the
interests of a deeper, purer understanding of
. . . of what? Everyone but the Hebrews held
that there were many gods, including the
Hebrew one, if one chose to say so; but the
Hebrews—Jacob (and his sons) like his father
before him, and his father before him—
maintained that there was only one god.
Only one god, who was God, and there was
no other. That was what made the Hebrew
family so unpopular with other people,
however much they might hide it much of
the time, except for a few people here and
there, like Hirah for instance, the Adullamite.
As for herself, well, she had lived with them
all her adult life, as had Judah's deceased wife,
of course, who indeed had met him at Hirah's
house, so she, Tamar, understood them better
than did most people. But she couldn't say it
had made for a happy life. Far from it. The
only thing was, there was something,
something, about Jacob mainly, that held her
in awe. It wasn't just his grand manner of a

successful patriarch, there was something, yes, there was something after all ineffable about him. You could see it in his eyes. He seemed to be living in tune with the very heavens, somehow. Oh, she knew people would say it was all nonsense. Life went on in its own sweet way as always. We were just insects born to live and die, etc. etc. And yet this old man . . . . Well, he seemed to be seeing something else as he looked at you. It wasn't that he was rude or thought himself superior. He served his god, he said. He had to serve his god. Only his god was God! In a queer way, it was as though the whole universe circled about Jacob, rather than that he was just an item in it. No, that was the wrong way to put it. It would make Jacob very angry to have that said of him. But the fact was, if his god, if God, were the centre of the universe, then Jacob was the only one in the world to know it, and such knowledge constituted a kind of divinity in itself. Besides, had he not fought with an angel, whatever that might mean?

"What price, lady?"

It was Judah! Come upon her whilst she was musing upon other things, though the baaing of sheep was now loud about her, and the animals hurried past like the waves of a muddy sea, their brown fleeces seeming to fountain up from the ridge of their bony backs and to fall at each side with a graceful swinging motion, their little hooves at the end of thin trotting legs rattling upon the baked earth. She must disguise her voice. This was surely the hardest part. Would he know her? From the depths of her throat and muffled by her veil a womanly voice, strangely seductive indeed, came forth.

"What will you give me, master?"

He hesitated. What was it? Did he not believe the voice? Did he recognise it? But no, it was not that. Something moved him. It wasn't desire, though he had approached her with that in his heart. It was fear. Not fear of her exactly, but fear of the consequences of what he was doing. Strange that he should hesitate for that. Had he not lain with a whore before?

She marked his hesitation and feared he would leave her without the embrace she desired. "What will you give me, master?" she repeated more insistently.

It was as though she compelled him now, but he was an experienced man, mature, haughty. Surely he did not have to go in unto her if his spirit would deny her? There would be plenty of prostitutes at the fair.

"What is it, master? Am I not desirable to you? Do you fear me?"

"You are comely enough, I dare say," he managed to reply, "though I do not expect to see your face, as your dedication to the goddess precludes it, but—"

She stood up, gracefully rearranging her robes as though it were part of a subtle dance of ambiguous meaning. "Well, Hebrew," she said, tossing her head proudly upward to meet his gaze directly, though he could not see her eyes, "do you have no taste for a Canaanite woman?"

He supposed she correctly guessed his origin from the colour of the sheep his servant was now driving past, or perhaps something in his speech or dress identified him as a Hebrew, though he was a settler of the fourth generation.

"My own wife, but recently dead," he quietly answered, "was a Canaanite woman."

"I'm sorry," she replied, with respect, "then perhaps you would not wish to know another just yet. But you stopped beside me."

"I will give you a kid from my herd of goats, to be sent you by the hand of my servant, if you will lie with me," he said without further ado.

She looked at him, slyly, he thought, by the inclination of her head. Now she was silent.

"Well?"

"I don't know you, master," she told him, in a wheedling tone. "Perhaps you will deceive me. Perhaps you will enjoy my body, leave me, and I shall not hear of you again. Or, what is more to the point, hear of the kid you promise me."

He bridled. "Do you call me a liar?" he cried.

A provoking laugh escaped her, totally fearless. "If I wished to call you a liar, master, I would call you one straight out, not by implication. No, it's just that not knowing you, for all I do know you may be a liar. Look here, master, this is what I'll do. Give me a pledge. Something I can identify you by and that you will know you have given me, so that there shall be no misunderstanding. Something you would like to be returned to you and something that wouldn't be much good to me. I mean something that I couldn't easily trade with someone else because they would be handling something, as you might say, hot. I'll tell you what. Give me that seal which hangs about your neck, and the cord it hangs from, and that staff in your hand."

"You ask for much," he answered, jibbing.

She reassumed her seat. "Well, that's my offer."

Judah did not know why he should consent to such a hard bargain with the woman, but he did. It was as though he couldn't help himself. Lechery, he thought, was a most powerful master, if it *was* lechery. He didn't know.

"Come with me," she said.

She took him into the cluster of drab buildings which formed the township of Ena'im, where men sat listlessly about the streets or occupied themselves mending various tools or household utensils, and women went by with amphorae balanced on their heads, whilst children played, and hungry dogs came sniffing for food. At least the deep shade was a relief after Judah's long treck from Hebron. At last they turned into an alley by which was reached the house in which a room had been set aside for Tamar's use, but not a soul was to be seen or heard anywhere on the premises. This had been a condition of Tamar's renting it, for which she had had to pay dear.

First, she bade him make himself comfortable, showing him the ewer and bowl, and the place for sanitation, whilst she went elsewhere to prepare herself. In a little while she came back with a platter of dates and a pitcher of wine, which she gave him, then stood back respectfully waiting; but he offered her a goblet of wine, that she might share with him. Not wishing to disturb her veil she politely refused, still standing in his presence, whilst he lay at his ease on a couch covered with splendid cloths. When he had finished, he beckoned to her, and she approached.

This was to be a matter of business for her, a stratagem to regain her rights, to win a husband who had been wrongfully denied her; and for him it was to be a matter of mere carnal pleasure, no more than drinking wine or eating rich food. He held out his arms to her, but his hands trembled as they touched her body; and she felt herself ache with desire. She was almost ashamed. Here was this man, her father-in-law, the sire of her two dead husbands, and it was as though it had been he she had wanted from the first! To conquer his unaccountable fear of her he pulled her roughly on to her side beside him, and brusquely lifted her robes until he felt the warm flesh beneath, whilst she fumbled with his own clothing. He was afire though, his fear lost in the tempestuous rush of desire that was met by an unaccountably equal rush of hers. This was no ordinary whore, he understood; and this was no ordinary client. So they strove in the heat and deep gloom of the chamber, till he lay exhausted upon her, and she panted wildly in the throes of her passion, clasping him fiercely until the strange lovely languor of the aftermath engulfed them both. She knew she had conceived, though there was no way of knowing. And he knew it too. For what had happened between them was the upshot of destiny, governed by the forces which moved

in the empty spaces of the grazing lands and
of the sky.

As soon as Judah was gone, she stowed his
pledges carefully away in a bundle, so that
they could not be seen, and got herself ready
to return to her father's house, changing out
of her harlot's dress and back into the
mourning clothes she habitually wore. Then,
as the sun went down, two strangers
mounted on mules and leading a third mule
arrived at the house. Tamar gave the men
food and drink, and showed them where they
could feed and water the mules, after which
all three quietly left Ena'im.

The bonfires were blazing at Timnah, and
a multitude of men and beasts were gathered
under the starlight. It was the evening of the
following day, after the great shearing was
done. Fleeces lay in mountainous heaps
everywhere, and merchants were still
bartering for them, whilst carcases were
roasting on spits and wine was flowing.
Women's voices were raised in laughter and
song, and the brilliant dyes of the materials
they wore were set off against the darkness,
like subtler shades of the bonfire flames, or
like flames fed with crystals that turned them
blue or green. In the centre of the open space
was a mighty figure upon which shadows and
light flickered so swiftly and so intensely that

it seemed itself to have movement and breath.

Judah and Hirah, with several others, staggered about the place, bumping into strangers, quarrelling, laughing, singing. There were women hanging about them.

The god seemed to be well satisfied. He sat there, observing all, with apparent benevolence. Not a word of protest or complaint did he utter. But then neither did the god of the Hebrews, so far as Judah knew, for he didn't hear Him or see the angry features of His face. For all Judah knew, God was as content to see His children enjoying themselves as any indulgent father might be, so long as there was no maiming, no killing. What did it matter if they got drunk, rioted a little, copulated, swore, gorged themselves on meat and threw away fruit which happened to be only slightly blemished? Wasn't the banquet of the earth spread for God's children? The poor-spirited might refrain out of some misbegotten fear, afraid perhaps of themselves, afraid to abandon themselves to pleasure in case they found themselves incapable of enjoying it, like men afraid to copulate in case they found they were impotent or in case they feared the contempt of unsatisfied women. Those poor souls deserved to suffer. They should be treated like the dogs they were—kicked!

They brought insult upon themselves. Could God sympathise with these creatures? No, they were lepers, spiritual lepers. And this self-imposed asceticism usually went with physical cowardice, too. They so clung to life, these vermin, to life that was as tasteless as meat without salt, that they were willing to undergo any humiliation rather than suffer pain or relinquish life altogether.

Jacob did not much indulge himself, though. He had his wives and his concubines, it was true; but he was a sober man. Perhaps not much fun! And he had been romantically in love. Did he not serve his uncle, Laban, fourteen years only that he might have Rachel to wife? But he, Judah, was a son of Leah "the tender eyed"; he did not spring from the romantic couple. And as for God, the god of the Hebrews, the One God, what could He do to save Joseph, his father's favourite? They had cast him into a waterless pit and the lad had vanished. Well, he certainly hadn't returned home. He, Judah, had suggested they sell him into slavery, but when Reuben went off to drag him out of the pit, he wasn't there! Well, that was certainly a mystery, but it didn't argue the displeasure of God or even His power. The lad had been insufferable with his vanity and pretence of innocence, but, what was perhaps even worse, he stole the old man's love away from the other, more mature sons. Jacob was perhaps at the beginning of his dotage. But it rankled, it rankled. "The sun and the moon and the eleven stars made obeisance to me"!

Judah drank more wine, to forget. There was nothing wrong with that, was there?

The figure of the god shimmered with flickering light and shadows, waves of light and shadow running upward, like creatures almost, yet rendering the image substance-less, as though it had dissolved into a liquid, a sort of waterfall plunging upward, to Heaven perhaps, or a vapour; and people, more and more people, were gathering about it. The whoops of revelry had died down. Masses and masses of people gathered before the image, which went on impassively flowing upward with light and shadow. A space was cleared and six masked figures began to dance to the rhythm of clashing sticks and stones rattled in a box, and then a single voice, a woman's, rose plaintively in the air, very beautiful, very sorrowful. The dancers went on as though unaware of it, though it was clearly all part of the same ritual. Judah gazed, bleary-eyed, from his vantage-point. The climax of the celebrations was approaching—the thanksgiving to the god for the plentiful fertility of the flocks. Seven rams were sacrificed. The crowd was now jubilant. And then a young man was led out with his hands tied behind him. Judah jumped down from his perch and hurried away.

When Judah got back to Hebron he bethought himself of the kid he owed to the prostitute at Ena'im, and he was anxious for the recovery of his pledge, so he quickly sent a servant back to the place, with a fine kid in his charge. But the servant could not find the woman. "What, a prostitute here, a votary, at Ena'im? There isn't one. But if you fancy something a little less grand, I can put you in touch with—" When it was clear that Judah's servant was not interested in just any whore, so that his informant did not stand to make any commission out of the matter, he told the servant that there had been such a votary, at the time of the sheep-shearing, but that she had gone away again, rather mysteriously it was true. But he did know which house it was where she had rented a room. For a little consideration the man pointed Judah's servant in the direction of the alley. But the crabbed old woman who seemed to be in charge there told him bluntly that there had never been any prostitute in her house—if it was her house—and she didn't intend to stand there being insulted by a total stranger and obviously one of very inferior birth. In short, no matter how hard he tried and no matter whom he asked, Judah's servant drew

an absolute blank at Ena'im, and so returned,
goat in tow, to his master's house. Judah was
very angry. He cursed the fellow for not
being industrious enough; he threatened to
put him on short commons; but gradually he
began to see that the man was telling the
truth. It was just no good. The woman had
vanished—with his seal, its cord, and his
staff: symbols of his high degree. But if he
were to institute a major search he might
open himself to ridicule in the eyes of those
who knew him, and that would bring
discredit on Jacob too, none of which would
do any good for his (Judah's) standing in the
world. So he decided to let the matter drop
for the time being, hoping that the woman
wouldn't use the pledges for purposes of
blackmail or to raise money by their sale: but
he had calculated on her not doing that when
he had parted with them, in the knowledge
that they were "hot " property and so likely
to be traced back to their owner who would
have the power of punishing her, probably by
death. So he decided to sit tight.

Normal life—the supervision of
dependants as well as of live and dead stock,
the discussion of domestic and general affairs
with his father and those of his brothers he
was more intimate with, amorous encounters
with his concubines and others, feasting
within the limits set by his pious father, and

even speculation as to the meaning of all the passion and business of life—occupied Judah as the months wore on; and he began to think about another marriage, now he had sufficiently, he thought, mourned for his late wife, Shua's daughter. However that might be, something occurred to disturb the relative calm of his days. Rumour had it that Tamar, his daughter-in-law, the one who was a thorn in his flesh, had become pregnant! If that were true, then she had brought irredeemable disgrace on them all. Wasn't she supposed to be in perpetual mourning, too: at least until she had married his son Shelah (which God forbid!)? The woman must be fetched before him at once. Had he not had enough worries of late without this calamity? Nay, she had killed two of his sons. Was she about to destroy the very House of Jacob? Judah's wrath knew no bounds.

So the hapless woman was brought before him, humble, fearful, still in widow's weeds, and, by her own account, three months pregnant. She was obliged to account for herself before a numerous assembly—the sons and daughters-in-law of Jacob with their older children, and various neighbouring notabilities with their wives and older children—for scandal of this kind needed to be publicly denounced, so as to be a deterrent to other wrongdoers. Judah was

not usually puffed up with self-importance
but on this occasion he was, because he sat
there with the memory of Er and Onan in his
mind, as well as the bad conscience mixed
with satisfaction that emanated from his
handling of the Shelah-Tamar affair.

"Well, Tamar, daughter-in-law," he said
bitterly, "what have you to say?"

"I have been guilty, my lord, of
fornication."

Hostile murmurs swept through the
crowd.

Judah felt the blood burn in his face, his
temples throbbed.

"I shall not have it!" he shouted. "How
dare you shame our House?"

There was no reply.

"I ask you again," he cried: "How dare
you shame our House?"

After a pause she answered, her voice too
low for many of those present, other than
Judah, to hear: "I have not shamed your
House."

"What?!" cried her incensed judge. "She
says she hasn't brought shame on the House
of Jacob!" he bawled out, so not a soul could
claim not to have heard. "She hasn't brought
shame on the House of Jacob!" he bawled
out again. "She has fornicated with some
unknown wretch and stained the marriage
bed of her two dead husbands, my sons, Er

and Onan. And she expects," he cried even louder, "to marry my third son Shelah, to whom she is betrothed! Never! Never!"

Tamar, kneeling at his feet, remained with her head bowed, silent.

"You know what your punishment will be, do you not, woman?" he asked her, in a more restrained voice.

"If I have brought shame on the House of Jacob, by fornication with one who had no right to know me in that way, then I am prepared for my just punishment," she answered in a clear voice, which kindled admiration in the breasts of those who heard her, for her courage if for nothing else.

Even Judah was moved, and half inclined to exercise clemency; but, once Tamar was out of the way, his anxiety about Shelah would be at an end, though, with the guilt upon her, it's true that she would no longer have any claim on either him or Shelah. But who was the man, her despoiler?

Vacillating between severity and mercy, he asked her to name the partner of her misdemeanour.

"I would rather," she said, "name him privately."

Not everyone present heard her reply, but those who did not soon got a report of it from those who did, causing a general subdued clamour.

"Tell me who was responsible, together with you, for your present plight!" roared Judah, made angry both by her ingratiating reply and by the disorder it had provoked.

"Very well!" she said, boldly rising to her feet, and bringing certain articles out from under the folds of her robe.

Judah stared. The assembled people, aghast at Tamar's insolence and yet hungry to know what the significance of the objects was, rose too. A gasp from the throats of those nearest the dais on which Tamar stood before the seated Judah signified that the objects had been identified by them.

"By the man, whose these are, am I with child!" she cried. Then, more quietly, to Judah alone: "Discern, I pray thee, whose are these, the signet, and the cords, and the staff!"

Judah hung his head; then, rising to his feet, declared before all the assembly: "She is more righteous than I; forasmuch as I gave her not to Shelah my son."

In course of time Tamar (a date-palm, as the Hebrew has it) gave birth to twins, Zerah and Peretz; and Peretz became one of the ancestors of King David.

Printed in the United Kingdom
by Lightning Source UK Ltd.
127501UK00001B/10-48/P